The
Applicant

The
Applicant

Nazlı Koca

corsair

CORSAIR

First published in the United States in 2023 by Grove Press
First published in the United Kingdom in 2023 by Corsair

1 3 5 7 9 10 8 6 4 2

Copyright © 2023, Nazil Koca

The moral right of the author has been asserted.

A CIP catalogue record for this book
is available from the British Library.

This book was designed by Norman E. Tuttle

HB ISBN: 978-1-4721-5810-9
TPB ISBN: 978-1-4721-5811-6

Printed and bound in Great Britain by Clays Ltd, Elcograf S.p.A.

Papers used by Corsair are from well-managed forests
and other responsible sources.

Corsair
An imprint of
Little, Brown Book Group
Carmelite House
50 Victoria Embankment
London EC4Y 0DZ

An Hachette UK Company
www.hachette.co.uk

www.littlebrown.co.uk

To Whom It May Concern,

I obey, I work, I appreciate. I scrub, I vacuum, I mop. I want you so bad I'll do whatever you ask.

I can kill, I can steal, I can take the blame for anything you need. I can dance, I can sing, I can be your exotic queen. I can carry, I can build, I can drive you from building to building. I can be the star of your football team. I can fight all your wars for a tiny shiny coin. Two coins and I will proudly work in your rotten hospitals, universities, tech companies. I can live in your apartments and take care of your babies. For free. It would be an honor to live under the same roof as you, your creepy husband, and your newborn baby. I can be your cheap prostitute, right here, right now, I can take it all in. If the earth collapses in on you one day, take this oath, I will be your human shield.

Will you let me stay, let me stay, let me stay.

August 15

Today I started working as a cleaner at a hostel. I'm not officially registered to work yet because of my visa status. Well, not really. I'm not registered because I still haven't sent them a copy of my visa, because I'm afraid they'll think my status is complicated.

But this has nothing to do with cleaning toilets. Or it has everything to do with it.

The hostel's name is Looking Glass. Dusty kitsch portraits of Alice, the Mad Hatter, and the queen hang on its sky-blue walls. It says "we're all med heir" in ugly letters down one whole side of the room, and there's a huge kaleidoscope mirror on the other.

When I walked in, a couple of pale and tall people, tattooed and pierced, were behind the bar, which is also the reception desk, talking about their wild weekends. I asked for Ali, my trainer for the day. I found him in the storage room, which is also the changing room. Ali is a Turkish graduate student who works three extra jobs so he can afford to be an unpaid lecturer at a university here. He's a barista, a delivery guy, and a cleaner. We kind of look alike, except we don't. Well, we're both Turkish and we both have dark hair.

First, we looked up how many checkouts there were today, using the company app on the androids assigned to us. Then we went to the Putzkammer to fill up our cleaning baskets.

Things we must put in our cleaning baskets:
Yellow cleaning cloths for the shelves in each room
Yellow sponges (or were they pink?)
Blue cloths and blue sponges for sure, for the toilets
Tea towels, also for the toilets
Mops
An empty Ikea bag for the dirty mops
Two spray bottles, one blue, one pink (first pink,
      then blue, like ladies first)

"Welcome to the bottom of the immigrant hierarchy," Ali said, handing me a pair of yellow latex gloves. He explained how at the end of every shift we must refill the spray bottles and put them on the shelves where they belong. We must put each dirty sponge, cloth, and tea towel into its own dirty basket. We must throw used bedsheets and bath towels into the laundry room through the little window in the basement. If we find anything that looks valuable, we must take it to the lost and found basket behind the reception. But if we find small things like bottles with Pfand, shampoos, or food left in the common kitchens after the guests have checked out, we can take them home. In Ali's words, they're our "treasures to keep."

Treasures of the day:

One shampoo

One shower gel

Five tampons

Half of the Pfand money (3.15 euros) we made recycling the bottles we found in the rooms

Finally, he said that all Putzis get two free beers at the end of each shift. I knew this already. If Looking Glass weren't the only place that had responded to my job application in months, this would've been a deciding factor. I'd visited Defne at the hostel a couple of times before she quit working here to start working at my old company, which I warned her many times against, but she didn't listen. She's now monitoring Turkish social media for child pornography and self-harm alerts and getting paid 4 euros per hour more than I am. She thinks it's worth it. Maybe it is, if you don't mind hating yourself, your country, and humanity so much that you'd rather do anything else for money than to ever go back there.

I had my free beers with Ali, so on my way home I was slightly drunk. As I walked to the U-Bahn, passing by all the party people, the homeless, the dealers, I thought of the first time I walked on Warschauer Strasse five years ago. I was only twenty-one. A Bavarian backpacker I'd met online picked me up from the S-Bahn and walked me to his squat house to spend the night. It was my first visit to Berlin and the first time I ever traveled on my own. Was it the thrill of being so far away from Turkey that kept me warm in his makeshift home in that slate-gray Berlin winter? Was it love at first sight with Berlin?

From what I'd gathered watching and rewatching *Christiane F.*, *Wings of Desire,* and *Berlin Calling* over the years, Berlin had seemed like a city where one wouldn't have to give up on her dreams to stay alive—especially if that dream was to hop into a bulldozer and demolish herself, a haunted house, one room at a time. And the moment I saw that Berlin was not a film set but a real, dark, and thrilling home to so many vagabonds, I knew I'd make it my home. I'd build a new Leyla here and hide her from eyes that knew us before, voices that wouldn't stop telling us what we could not do. And I did it. I moved here less than a year after that cold November night.

I came here to write. I'd known I wanted to be a writer before I knew how to read, but after college, I found myself only writing copy for advertising agencies that sucked all creativity out of me. Life was so expensive and politics so erratic in Turkey that all of my attempts at literary writing were shut down for one reason or another, each time leaving me with less courage to say what was on my mind. I was turning into Joyce's Bloom, walking the streets of Istanbul like a ghost, unable to reconcile how far my reality was from the dreams I once had. There was more hope for Stephen Dedalus in Dublin than for me in Istanbul. But Berlin was going to be different. If there was anything I'd heard more about this city than its unmatched freedoms, it was that anyone could afford a decent life here on a part-time job's salary. Universities were free for everyone. I'd enrolled in a master's program for the visa and found a student job in my first week. I moved into a shared Altbau apartment in Neukölln and met other aspiring writers in bars where taboos didn't seem to exist.

I was so intoxicated by Berlin that I didn't even smell the puke, the piss, the poverty. Punks smoking and fighting, drunk, seemed like real-life Renaissance paintings of biblical miracles to me. It took me six years to realize that not everyone on the streets of Berlin was there by choice. I was such a Dummkopf. I still am. I'm still in love with this filthy city, but now I know that Berlin's love isn't free.

I'm going to keep the cleaning job a secret from my mother and sister. They have enough to deal with in Turkey. I don't want them to remember the days when we had a cleaner and give them yet another reason to be sad about the way our lives have changed. Our cleaner, Fatma Teyze, might have been my mother's closest friend. Once, my mother decided to break up with my father and told my sister to drive us all to Fatma Teyze's house, because she didn't trust any of her other friends to keep her secret. We stayed in Fatma Teyze's house for half an hour and then my father picked us up. Fatma Teyze was back at her job in our home the next Tuesday, and we never spoke of that night or a breakup again.

But I never forgot the taste of the kaçak tea that burned my tongue while we all sat quietly in Fatma Teyze's small kitchen, the sound of football coming from their TV in the living room and her husband pretending to watch the game but giving Fatma Teyze angry looks behind my mother's back, as if to say, *You'll pay for this once they leave. And they better leave soon.*

I've been watching Turkish TV on my laptop since I got home from work today. My soap opera addiction is getting serious. But I have no money to go out to try and fight it.

While the Turkish Coca-Cola commercial did a close-up on a happy family gathering around a big table to have baklava and Coke after a long day, I said, "Alexa, start cleaning," and my roommate Victor's Roomba started motoring around the floor. I cleaned the fallen leaves of the only plant in our flat and decorated it with strips of paper I ripped from an old art magazine as if it were a wishing tree to hang dreams on Hıdırellez. Victor came out of his room to cook and said, "Alexa, play some jazz music." I slunk back to my room, quietly, like Gregor Samsa in *The Metamorphosis* after realizing no one wanted him in the living room, carrying my soap opera friends with me inside my laptop screen.

This show's called *Uzak*. The son of a rich, traditional Turkish family is away from home, studying medicine in Berlin. In the beginning, we learn that he's had a great setup here for years, living in a stylish loft in West Berlin with a German model. Though of course the soap quickly makes us root for a Turkish girl instead, who grew up in a village with an alcoholic and violent father who sold her to be married to the rich boy when she was a baby. When her father died, she moved to Istanbul for college, thinking she was finally free, that her life was saved by the big city, just like how the rich boy felt in Berlin, unaware of his father's plans for his future. They were both fools to think that they could escape the lives their families wrote out for them. Halfway through the first episode, they were already married and the girl had fallen in love with the boy, who left her alone in Berlin to spend the summer in the US with his model girlfriend. Alone in Berlin, the Turkish girl started to hang out with Turkish German hustlers who lived down the street from where I live, Kottbusser Tor, and sending photos of "home-cooked" meals to her in-laws from a Turkish restaurant, which in real life is Syrian, but okay. In the final scene, she lies to them about being pregnant so the boy can't break up with her when he returns from the US like he said he would. It's exhausting to be alone in Berlin, faking oneself to your family back home and another to the people around you. But she will make it work. We all do. I've talked to my mother and sister on the phone every single day since I moved here, but they had no idea how close I'd come to annihilation until a couple months ago.

For the most part, neither did I.

I found this notebook under the couch. Someone must've forgotten it in my room because I don't remember buying it at all. It's not me: it's orange. I hate orange. And it has thick, white pages. Or who knows? Maybe this is me now: whatever I find on the floor. Whatever I can have. Nothing I want.

I'm going to write in this notebook every day.

I probably won't. I was never able to keep a diary for longer than a week. I was never able to finish anything I started. I know I finished some things, but it sure doesn't feel like it right now. After spending the whole day learning the art of cleaning, all I can see now is the dust in the corners that the Roomba can't reach, Victor and Heidi's fallen hair all over the bathroom entangled with mine, and the stains I never noticed before on every mirror I turn to.

August 18

Last night I dreamed that Mona was back in Berlin. (Mona was my best friend—until one day she left the country without saying a word. I only found out she was gone later, once she settled into her new life in LA, as if we had been no more than two acquaintances, friends of friends.) (I guess that's exactly what we were. I was a friend of one of Mona's many invented selves, as she was mine.) The dream Mona was beautiful as ever with her big black eyes, pixie hair, and striped crop top. She worked at the hostel too. We cleaned the dream lobby together, which was in a garden with an enormous palm tree in its center, where Mona and I were sharing a long, black clove cigarette. She wanted us to rob the hostel safe and run away.

"Where to?" I asked.

"LA, London, wherever we want," she said. "Somewhere you can write stories and I can read all day."

Mona had come to save me from selling my hands, my feet, my back for 8.5 euros an hour. I was overcome with relief—until she said we needed to do something radical to distract people.

Not the tree, not the tree, I thought.

"The tree," she said. "We'll light the tree on fire. Once everybody comes out, we'll go in and empty the safe."

There'll be more palm trees in LA, I thought. I've never been there but I've seen enough series set in LA to give dream Leyla the confidence to assume that.

Mona said she'd start the fire if I wanted to search the rooms for any treasures worth taking. As I went in and out of private rooms and common kitchens, I started doubting whether I wanted to leave Berlin. I found more treasures than I could fit in my Ikea bag: bottles of Berliner Kindl, dozens of Kinder Surprise, a large bag of coke, and finally a 500-euro bill. I ran to the garden to show Mona all that I'd found. I wanted to tell her we didn't have to burn the tree. We didn't have to steal anything.

But I woke up before I could find Mona. I don't know if dream Leyla was able to save the tree. I also don't know why dream Leyla thought she could go to London or LA, when I barely have a visa to be in Berlin. I don't know what made me dream of Mona after all this time. I haven't spoken to her in months. I didn't write anything when she texted me saying she'd moved to the US. What could I have said? If she wanted to tell me why she left, she would have.

I've known that I couldn't make Mona tell me anything real unless she wanted to herself since the first time I met her in that deathly toilet stall in Sisyphos, buying drugs from the same dealer. We were both on our own and high out of our minds. She said she was Canadian, but she had an ambiguous look and accent, like me. She also said she was older than I was, but she looked a couple years younger. After snorting the first line, she told me she was actually from France and four years younger than me.

When I asked her why she lied, she shrugged; it was an old habit.

"I usually don't talk to anyone long enough to feel like I owe them the truth," she said.

We stayed together for the rest of the party because the dealer only had one tube of ketamine left to sell; he suggested we share it. Retrospectively, it's not hard to see that we could have easily split the powder in the tube, gone our separate ways. We were both equally lonely. But I only came to know her well-concealed desolation much later. For a long time, we remained distant party friends. She would come to my apartment or wherever I was when she called at odd hours, but she never invited me to her place or introduced me to her friends. I didn't pay this any attention at first, back when I attended classes at the university and had a part-time office job. Time passed clandestinely when I believed that Berlin loved me back.

Who wouldn't have believed it? Mona had even written it on the street once, right by the entrance of Görlitzer Park. She'd spray-painted a birthday cake and written "happy birthday leyla! berlin loves you!" under it. She'd pulled me away from my apartment (where I had a dozen guests) at 3:00 a.m., covered my eyes with her hands, and walked me over to the park, where she told me to open my eyes and popped open a bottle of Rotkäppchen. I told Mona on the way back to my apartment that up until that moment, I couldn't have imagined feeling so happy. Doubtless ketamine played a part in reaching that level of bliss, but still.

Now, I wonder who had to clean after us the next day. Who had to repaint the ground and bring Berlin back to its brutal gray?

Yesterday I had my second training shift at the hostel. My trainer for the day was Mia, who's an Italian DJ, photographer, graphic designer, and cleaner. She also looks like me, except she's taller, older, and has fake eyebrows, I think.

"So," she asked me while we took our cleaning baskets to the first room, "how did you end up here?"

I told her about how I was kicked out of the university for writing a thesis that wasn't academic enough, how I begged my professor to let me pass because my visa depended on it, how he said, "That is not my problem. If you are not happy with my decision, sue me." I told Mia about how I sued him—and the whole university—appealing for a reevaluation or a chance to write a new thesis and how I now have to wait for the court to decide what happens next on a Fiktionsbescheinigung (as in fictional certificate), which allows me to neither enroll in another program nor start a full-time job.

"Asshole!" Mia said, like everyone else who heard this story in the last three months.

Everyone says that they've never heard of anyone failing their thesis before. "Who does that to someone?" they ask. I don't know. I don't want to talk about it anymore. I don't want to think about being the only one anyone has ever heard of who has failed their thesis.

After I told Mia the whole story, I realized that I hadn't told Ali any of it. Partly because he talked rather than listened but mostly, and undeniably, because it's much more difficult to talk about failure in Turkish. It triples the pain, the shame, the drama of real life to think in that language. Because I lost everything I had in Turkish. Because I cried for all my losses in that white room called mother tongue, a white windowless room in the psych ward called the past. And even the way you cry changes when you leave your mother's side. You learn to cry quieter, and it starts hurting less. Or maybe it doesn't hurt less at all. Maybe you simply give up on the idea that crying can soothe your pain when there's no one to tell you everything will be okay in the room. Or maybe I don't want anyone to tell me everything will be okay in the language of my childhood because my childhood room is where I learned that nothing in this world would ever be okay.

I asked Mia why she was working at Looking Glass.

"I needed to do something I didn't care about," she said. "A job that wouldn't consume my brain so I could focus on my art. Cleaning was the perfect match. It's good exercise too."

She told me that most cleaners at the hostel were artists and often collaborated on projects. But when I told her I was a writer, she didn't bother to ask what kind. Was it because I wasn't dressed like a Berlin artist (my pants were black but my T-shirt was white) (and I don't own any combat boots) or could she tell from my eyes that I haven't written anything new in over a year? I figured it was a combination of both and didn't tell her that I had a couple of essays up on Berlin's most popular websites or that I was once a sought-after reader at bar poetry nights. Or that though I haven't put out any new work in a while, I've found other ways to collaborate with artists she must have heard of. What did it matter? I was at the Looking Glass to learn how to be a cleaner not to prove myself as a writer. I'd had twenty-six years to do that, but instead I'd ended up in that training session with Mia, which was apparently just as doomed as my writing career.

Mia was supposed to watch me clean, but I was so slow that we had to split the rooms to be able to finish on time. I thought I did fine, but it turns out I broke a drain and messed up cleaning one bathroom. Today, the head of the maids messaged me twice to tell me about the chaos I caused: the guests complained, and the hostel had to give them their money back.

My mother kept calling me while I was trying to figure out whether this meant I was fired, and whether I fucked up because I subconsciously wanted to get fired, or if I was simply incapable of doing anything right. I knew she wouldn't stop calling until I answered, so I picked up when she called for the sixth time. She asked if everything was okay. I said yes. She said I sounded sad. I said I was okay. She asked if I was sure. "Ya! Üf!" I groaned. I hung up. Then I opened the free beer I brought home from the hostel and drank it on my own.

I apologized, and the head of the maids liked my message on the app.

August 20

Today I went to the Ausländerbehörde to consult a lawyer who gives free immigration advice once a month, a young Syrian who spoke fluent Turkish, German, and English. He smelled like lemon cologne.

I told him my story and asked what would happen if the court couldn't decide on my case until my Fiktionsbescheinigung expires in three months, three weeks, six days, and twelve hours.

He looked amused at first, then worried and curious. "Why are you so terrified of moving back to Turkey?" he asked. Did I have a reason that would make me eligible for asylum or refugee status?

I remembered a conversation I had on a plane with a middle-aged Turkish stranger. It was a few years ago, when I was flying back to Turkey from Copenhagen where I'd been visiting friends. He asked what I had been doing in Copenhagen, and five minutes later I found myself telling him about how I felt guilty because I'd just lied to a friend to cover up for her cheating girlfriend. Maybe because he wore all black and looked like a Muslim priest. He told me that I shouldn't be too hard on myself. He said it was normal to cheat in Denmark and then asked if I had a boyfriend with a grin that made him look like a different kind of priest entirely. I said yes, which was only partly true, and asked him how he moved to Copenhagen to reroute the conversation. When was it? What kind of visa did he get?

He said he was granted asylum by Denmark in the seventies. I felt bad for thinking less of him. I asked what he had to seek asylum from.

"Solcu muydunuz?"

He burst out laughing and said only an idiot would care about politics enough to drive himself to exile. He visited a cousin in Denmark the summer he graduated from high school and simply didn't want to go back. So, he made up a few lies about people wanting to kill him in Turkey and they let him stay. Back in the day, he said, it was as easy as that.

Today, the only asylum seekers I know are my Syrian party friends who I've met at Sisyphos. They might be partying and dealing drugs now, but they all crossed borders and seas, escaping mortar shells and Kalashnikov gunfire from their own government and people. The only Turkish asylum seekers I've heard of are writers, artists, and academics who would've been arrested if they hadn't run away. I've been hearing a lot of stories about Afghan refugees too. They're being sent back after years of living in Berlin because supposedly the war in their country is over. Many of them get killed as soon as they get off the plane.

So, no, I said to the Ausländerbehörde counselor. I don't have a reason to seek asylum. I have been too much of a coward to speak up against my government. I had one controversial essay up on a website, and I asked the editor to take it down when I thought I was getting kicked out of Germany in June. I know that I could lie and make a case for myself to stay here as a refugee, but I wouldn't be able to live here in peace knowing I took the place of a journalist or a trans person whose life is in real danger in their own countries.

Let's say I didn't care. When you are an asylum seeker or a refugee in Germany you aren't allowed to visit your home country. You lose your refugee status here if you do. And since my family can't afford to come here, I would be giving up on seeing them for years. So maybe this is the real reason why I won't apply for asylum. And maybe I don't really care about others.

Why can German cars, intelligence software, and pharma roam in Turkey more freely than they ever could in their own country, yet I can't have one room in Kreuzberg to watch soaps and contemplate writing in without having to choose between my conscience and asylum, my ideals and academia, my family in Turkey and freedom here?

The counselor asked if I had any friends who'd marry me. No? Four years in Berlin and no friends who care enough about me to marry me? No boyfriend? Did I have any money to pay someone? No. No. No. No.

"Maybe that's for the best," the counselor said. "I hear a lot of horror stories about visa marriages. The woman who was here before you, for example. She paid someone, a friend of a friend, to marry her. Everything went smoothly until they dealt with all the paperwork and she got her residency permit. As soon as they left the

Ausländerbehörde, the man turned around and said, 'Now, you will start paying me two thousand euros every month, or else I will tell the government this marriage is a fraud.'"

He didn't have any other advice for me. Except that I shouldn't even consider overstaying my visa since Europe is always looking for reasons not to let us in. He repeated what I already knew: I would get a five- to ten-year ban on applying for a new visa if I broke any rules, that I should stick to my job since the Ausländerbehörde will be checking my accounts for official and stable income, and that I should try to talk to my professor again or get a lawyer to have a higher chance at winning the appeal. But I can't afford a lawyer and if I see my professor again, I will have a breakdown and will definitely need a lawyer then. And probably a psychiatrist too.

The counselor went on to tell me about how Turkey is a great country, how Erdoğan is a strong leader, standing up to the West, opening his arms to the East. And that was my cue to leave.

I was still feeling out of sorts from my visit to the Ausländerbehörde, and the hostel hadn't called me in for my
next shift, so when Heidi knocked on my bedroom door
the next day holding a mirror with cute lines of speed and
the sound of techno rattling out of her laptop speakers,
it didn't take her long to convince me to pause my soap
and go out with her.

"Wanna go to Sisy?"

"I can't."

"Even if I pay for the entrance and the ketamine?"

I looked at her with my mouth open for a second—you
get this kind of invitation once in a lifetime in Germany—
but it wasn't a long second.

Heidi threw my dress on the bed. She didn't have to ask
what I would wear because I've been wearing the same
dress all summer—an old present from my mother—one
with deep, dark crimson roses. I put it on and brushed my
hair. Heidi already looked fine with her long red hair, jean
shorts, and tank top. She seems a little skinnier every time
I see her, which is not very often. She may as well be living in the clubs, and when she's not dancing in some dark
room, she's in Lichtenberg, trying to save her relationship
with her DJ boyfriend. We snorted a few lines at home
and took our Sternis with us to the train.

As soon as we arrived at Sisyphos, we found Felix, the most reliable dealer I've ever known. He's always dancing in front of the DJ in Hammerhalle with his fanny pack and chewing gum, moving his pale, skinny arms up and down behind his back like a moth. We got into the toilet stall with Felix and two other boys: one Lebanese, the other Liberian. All brought together by our shaman, Felix, who quickly left us in search of new followers, the four of us spent the rest of our club day together.

Zain was a tourist, visiting from Beirut for the weekend. An architect. Tall, handsome, friendly. Zain's muscular body was unmarked by Berlin. His bronze skin hadn't lost its glow. Heidi couldn't keep her eyes off him. He had a girlfriend back home and was not interested in Heidi, but Mohamed, the Liberian, was into Heidi. Of course, Heidi wasn't into Mohamed at all. Nobody was flirting with me, and I wasn't flirting with anyone. All I wanted was more speed, more ketamine, and cocaine. I couldn't stop thinking about cocaine as I danced, even though I could feel that the sober Leyla was in there somewhere, judging this parasite Leyla. One Leyla only wanted to keep dancing, one Leyla wanted to take an endless line of drugs, one Leyla wanted to sleep and not have to talk with anyone ever again.

Then, Mohamed grabbed the wrist of all Leylas at once and yelled into our ear.

"Follow me. I found a little bit of coke. Come. Coke."

His voice sent a shiver down my spine. He didn't invite the others, who were dancing side by side with a Berlin-proper distance and their eyes locked on the DJ. This, I figured, meant that he was tired of waiting for Heidi to give up on Zain, and he was going to try to hook up with me. I wasn't sure how I felt about that. I followed him.

We went into a secret room passing through a short labyrinth. No one was there, so we settled in. He made two huge lines. We snorted them. He made two more. I didn't need more but since they were there, I took another. He put his phone, credit card, and 5-euro bill in his pocket and his hands around me. He lifted me up and I kissed him, because why not I thought.

We had sex there for a while, at the center of the labyrinth, until we remembered we were high, and no one would come. It was a sad hit of awareness: we had both gone in there by choice, we took all the lines in excitement, we pulled and pushed our bodies onto one another with a sense of urgency, but once everything turned out as it would after those steps, we realized it was all for nothing. The fever was ersatz, there were no fluids left in our bodies—no spit, no come, no tears. We took more lines and went back to the dance floor.

The DJ played all the hypnosis songs, "Bringing Down Their System," "Deluge," "Insulated." We all danced, snorted, smoked, drank, and repeated for ten more hours. Occasionally we sat by the out-of-tune piano in the garden and told each other stories about our worlds outside.

"Don't you ever want to leave Lebanon?" I asked Zain.

"Never," he said. "Beirut is my home."

I asked him if he'd read *Les désorientés*, an Amin Maalouf novel I read when I still lived in Istanbul about a Lebanese man who had moved to France after the civil war. Decades pass and the man visits his homeland for the first time to see a dying friend who chose to cooperate with corruption and lived a prosperous life. I'd written a review of the book when it first came out in Turkey, but the website took it down promptly after the Gezi Park protests. They didn't give me an explanation. They didn't have to. I gave away my copy to the free library at the park that summer and picked up a copy of Camus's *The Rebel*, which I never ended up reading but carried with me all the way to Berlin, to this apartment.

"I don't like Maalouf," Zain said. "He writes for the West not the East."

"But isn't that like saying we're here to dance for the West and not the East? Couldn't he be writing for himself and everyone at once? Or what if he is stuck? What if he is both the East and the West inside?" I asked.

I realized only later how tightly I was holding his wrist, as if I could squeeze an answer out of him. But he wanted to go back to Felix, the toilet booth, the dance floor. When Zain left for Berghain on his own, Heidi, Mohamed, and I headed for our place.

The three of us stayed linked arm in arm the whole way. When we sat on my broken red velvet couch, Mohamed put his hand between my legs, and Heidi started playing with my hair.

Mohamed said he loved watching porn while coming down from drugs. Heidi put on a video of a woman who was masturbating while reading from *Henry & June*.

I told them I wasn't in the mood for a threesome.

"A threesome?" Mohamed asked, trying to look confused.

Heidi and I chuckled. Then she said, "Okay my dear," gave me a kiss on both cheeks, and went to her room.

Not only would it be stupid to engage in any sexual activity with my roommate (again), but also I barely have the energy to have sex with one person these days. I think I only brought Mohamed home so that I could lay my head on a man's chest.

I closed the video, put on Yusef Lateef's "First Gymnopédie," and told Mohamed I was ready for sleep. I said he could go hang out with Heidi if he wanted, but he got under the duvet with me.

There's something about a male body that puts me to sleep like no other downer. Heidi says it's hormones. I think it's because I've lost all hope that any man can tell me anything that I would want to stay awake to listen to.

August 25

I cleaned twelve rooms on my own today. No one brought up the broken drain.

Cleaning the first shower while the head of the maids watched my every move, I spilled bleach on my only pair of pants. Only then did I realize that everyone else changed their clothes when they came in. They all walk into the hostel in their Dr. Martens and shorts and change into Adidas sneakers and sweatpants in the bathrooms before they start cleaning. I only have one pair of shoes and my other pair of pants are my pj's. So, I'll go to work in my pj's from now on.

I'm hosting a talk with a minor Berlin celebrity tonight, but the shame of being lousy at cleaning gets to me. I both want to quit before I get fired and keep this job I need. I'm scared I'll fail at tonight's show too. I wonder how of much of this new insecurity I owe to cleaning toilets for a living.

Treasures of the day:
7 euros in Pfand money
Two pocket-size bottles of vodka
ja! pasta
ja! milk

August 26

Last night's show left me feeling even further away from the bold writer I thought I'd become by now.

I told Eve, the minor celebrity, to meet me at the U1 platform of Kottbusser Tor two hours before the show so that we could ride the U-Bahn from Warschauer Strasse to Uhlandstrasse back and forth, drinking wine, catching up. Eve's a thirty-year-old female empowerment vlogger with a million followers on Instagram. I know her from an old job at an online film magazine, which was so bad that it inspired her to start vlogging and left me incapable of writing for months. Our boss, Dmitri, would edit my writing, sending back notes like "this is too boring" or "too sentimental" or "too angry." His condescending accusations haunt me to this day.

When I wasn't working for Dmitri, I worked as a customer service agent to pay the bills, which didn't help my confidence. Eve was the editor in chief of the magazine but for a few weeks only. She got fired right after I got hired. Dmitri was an old Russian man who dressed like he was in his twenties and came to work once a week with a new young woman linked to his arm. He was a charming man who looked into your eyes when he spoke, opened doors, and lit up cigarettes for you with a permanent smile on his face—unless you were working for him.

Once, before we both got fired, Dmitri took me and Eve to Paris Bar on Kantstrasse. He told us about his plans to send us to fairs and conferences and festivals in Cannes, New York, and LA. He wanted to move the office from Kreuzberg to Mitte within a year and to open a bar under the office where he would name cocktails after his favorite movies like *Last Tango in Paris* or *Lolita*.

It wasn't a great sign that one of the movies he mentioned was basically a rape movie and the other one about a pedophile. (Although I have to confess I masturbated twice while reading *Lolita* last summer.) (Funny I should say "I have to confess" in my own diary.) But I pushed it to the back of my mind quickly. I really wanted to keep the job. I thought I was a feminist, but who knows what I thought that meant. I only knew Simone de Beauvoir as Sartre's partner. I was twenty-four. Besides, even Eve, who was four years older and four years more confident, hadn't said anything. She nodded and took a sip of her wine, smiled and took a long drag of her cigarette instead.

After she got fired, Eve left Berlin and moved to London. She disappeared from the face of the internet for a few months and one day reappeared as a vlogger. In her videos, she's sometimes half-naked, sometimes with full makeup, sometimes in her pj's with no makeup, sometimes at the hair salon, cooking, or taking care of a friend's baby as she talks about the power of femininity, why men are so scared of it, and the latest fashion trends.

She invited herself to be a guest on my show at Giovanni's Room, an apartment-turned-theater in Schlesi, where

I've been interviewing Berlin celebrities about how Berlin shaped their lives in front of an audience. Giovanni sells wine and beer for 3 euros each. We charge 5 euros for entry and give all that we earn to the featured artists. I don't get anything except free drinks, which is the last thing I need, I know.

I waited for Eve with a bottle of pinot noir in one hand and a poorly rolled cigarette in the other, looking at the neon lights of the city through the dirty glasses of the U1 platform. I thought of an old Turkish movie: a reinterpretation of *Faust* starring MFÖ. It's about a musician who sells his soul to the devil in exchange for fame. It's set in Istanbul in the eighties. I don't remember much else about the movie, other than the lights. The feeling of the neon: the world they made one a part of, as if the gas leaked out of first the signs and then the TV, addicting me to its high. The neon lights of Kottbusser Tor always remind me of a Turkey I never saw in real life. A Turkey where wishes could come true. In the Turkey I know, wishes die slower deaths than their makers, passing on from generation to generation, wilting everything they touch.

Eve showed up with a bottle in one hand and a cigarette in the other too. Her bottle was a Sekt, her cigarettes Vogues. We clinked our bottles and hugged. We stepped on our cigarettes at the same time when the train arrived. "Wait," she screamed before we got on the train and popped the Sekt open. Inside the train, I told her to pick the seats, since she was the guest. I pulled out two paper cups from my bag.

"So, tell me everything!" I said. "How's London? Your life looks so glamorous from here."

"Ha," she said and took a gulp from her bottle. "I only managed to survive in London for six months. I live with my mother now, in Poland."

Turns out, she saved photos and videos she took in London in those six months and has been sharing them from her high school bedroom in rural Poland for the last year and a half. She did make some money from her Instagram followers but not enough to afford to live in London. She made me promise not to tell anyone about it.

After going back and forth between Uhlandstrasse twice, we got off the train at Schlesi and went to the theater. Giovanni and Eve air-kissed one another and bonded right away over their matching vintage silk outfits. I pretended I had an urgent email to send and went backstage to play with Giovanni's sassy Bengal cat Sophia Loren until it was time for the show to start.

I miss the days when Giovanni and I were just friends. Ever since we started working together on the show, he's been acting like it's okay to give me orders and cut into my sentences. Maybe he feels he's stuck with me since the show was my idea, and he's trying to get me to quit so he can find someone more glamorous to be the host, someone without a bleach stain on her only pair of pants. Why else would he constantly try to give me *suggestions* on how to do a job I created for myself? He's not even paying me, and I never agreed for him to be the director of my show. But the thought of confronting him triggers a dangerous impulse in me. I'm afraid I'd end up shouting at him, tearing up, remembering all the times this impulse was triggered and suppressed since the last time I broke down, in Turkey. And though he's been living in Berlin for nearly three decades, my Mediterranean temper could wake Giovanni's Mediterranean temper, too, the one that he so carefully tries to hide behind his concocted American accent. Then, we could destroy what we have now, even though all the shows we did together have been hits. By hits I mean they all filled the room, which fits a maximum of fifty people. I bring new people to Giovanni's radar and Giovanni to theirs, and he gives me the room to investigate how to exist as an artist. None of the DJs, actors, or writers I interviewed would have agreed to it if I didn't offer them a seat on Giovanni's stage. There's something about Giovanni's Room that attracts the strong and singular. And there's something about me that gets them to open up—though I might be losing my charm.

Last night onstage, Eve answered all my questions using big words that said nothing. I asked about her Berlin years three times, but she kept bringing up London: how expensive but diverse it is, how rainy but eventful, how worth it because unlike Berlin if you work hard enough you'll get somewhere regardless of where you're from. *Somewhere like Instagram with a million followers or your mother's place in rural Poland?* I wanted to ask. I kept my promise, but as if to make up for Eve's lie, I told everyone who congratulated me after the show that I'm a cleaner.

And now I feel guilty about that, too, because I'm not a cleaner-cleaner. I could be admitted back to the university any day now. The court could decide that my thesis was good enough to pass, and I could become a master of arts overnight. Then, I would have eighteen months to find a real job, which should be more than enough, even though I don't know what I mean by a real job since I don't ever want to work in an office again. Is this why I am so eager to call myself a cleaner? Do I think that being a cleaner might make me a part of the city in a way neither being a student nor an artist could?

A poor immigrant who wants to create art is irrelevant. A poor immigrant looking for a good job is an annoyance. A poor immigrant looking for any job to survive has the potential to be profitable. But to turn a profit one needs to get rid of all the inconveniences like self-regard, hopes, and dreams. Only at this point can the most grateful immigrants stop being Ausländer and instead become synonymous with their jobs. Because what is a city but a department of a multibillion-dollar company called the state? If we don't have enough money to spend in its malls, we must work for it.

The fact is, whatever I want to call myself doing this job, the pay will be barely enough to survive. I'm only allowed to work part-time in Germany until my visa issues are resolved. Ausländerbehörde almost wasn't going to extend my visa because I couldn't prove where my previous income came from and went to. After years of networking, by which I mean applying for every gig posted on craigslist—from buying dozens of boxed milk powder and shipping it to Chinese mothers who don't trust their own country's milk products not to kill their babies to entertaining coke-fueled rock stars from distant countries in hotel rooms—I had somehow fashioned a semifunctional financial survival system here. But as the Angela Merkel look-alike Ausländerbehörde officer firmly reminded me before she handed me my Fiktionsbescheinigung in June, students on visas like mine are not allowed to work freelance in Germany. We're only allowed to work for German companies 120 days per year. Our only other income can be the allowance sent to us from our families, and the German government needs to know how we spend it. God forbid we'd send too much European money to Turkey.

I used to deposit the cash I made from whatever hustle I could find to my account the same day each month so that if anyone asked, I could tell them that my family sent me money with a relative who traveled here for work, when in fact I was the only one sending money to anyone whenever I could. I told the Ausländerbehörde my parents had more than enough money to support me. They just didn't know how to use online banking and were too old to walk to the bank. It worked but barely. The officer made a note on my file. She said unless I could show an official bank transfer from Turkey or a part-time job contract in Germany next time, I wouldn't be allowed to stay in the country whether I win the case against the university or not. Thus, into the Looking Glass.

At least the hostel lets us plan our own schedules, so I can work every day for two weeks and then not work at all for the rest of the month. Maybe if I don't have to chase an odd job to pay the rent all the time, I can finally write a novel—or at least learn German or how to ride a bike.

I deleted my Facebook, Instagram, and Twitter accounts when I woke up this morning. Not temporarily disabled. Deleted for good. No more lies.

(Only minor abstractions of truth when absolutely necessary.)

August 31

I went to Defne's after work last night. She lives near the mall in Prenzlauer Berg.

Before I left work, Ali insisted I should have beers with him and the other cleaners instead of hoarding them for a change. I said okay, since I also found a bottle of red, almost full, to take to Defne's. Ali found half a bottle of tequila, so we had a few shots of that too. Then he offered me a line of ketamine in the bathroom. I took it of course. But I hated being high on keta at the hostel. I had to leave immediately, as if getting my body out of Looking Glass for the day could fix my displacement. As if I had a place I belonged to that I could go back to. As if I could start walking again and arrive at the right place this time.

I took the S-Bahn to Schönhauser Allee. When I got there I really had to pee, so I went inside the mall. I almost ran to the toilet until a group of toilet cleaners stopped me at the entrance.

"Ein euro!" the man who sat behind a bowl of euros yelled.

I knew I shouldn't spend 1 euro just to pee. I should always pee in a corner outside like a real Berliner. I hadn't thought this through. Now, standing across from a bunch of toilet cleaners, the question was whether I would try and Turkish-talk my way out of paying for it. But wouldn't

I have to spend my 1 euro somewhere else if not here? Maybe a friend was going to borrow it the next day and never return it because he wouldn't realize how much 1 euro meant to me. Maybe I was going to lose it. Either way, I would feel guilty for not giving my euro to a fellow cleaner, whose job is no doubt harder than mine. So I put my euro into the bowl and went in to pee.

Half of the toilets had hair, pee, and shit stains in them. There were used toilet paper pieces on the floor. All the things I had to clean earlier in the day. At least in my job toilets make only a third of a day's cleaning responsibilities. Bedrooms can be filthy, too, filthier than bathrooms sometimes, but mostly they aren't. Now and then you even get a clean bedroom that smells nice. You can take a break there. You can forget how people forget you exist. How they leave behind all their dirt for you to pick up without caring to throw their used condoms into the trash can or at least tip you. Nobody tips the unseen.

On the way out, the toilet cleaners said to me, "Dankeschön, tschüss, guten abend."

I didn't want them to think that I was one of *them*, you know, a European with money who doesn't see them.

So, I said, way too cheerfully, "Ben de Türküm, ben de temizlikçiyim burada!"

We talked a little about our jobs and where we came from, but I left when one of them told me I didn't look alright. What was wrong with me?

Defne's place is fifteen minutes away from Schönhauser Allee but it took me almost forty minutes to walk there.

I took a right on the wrong street twice. When I finally arrived, Defne was cooking lentil soup, my favorite. I sat on her kitchen table, poured us two glasses of wine, started rolling two cigarettes from her tobacco. I haven't had enough to buy tobacco since my last bag ran out, but I don't crave cigarettes as much as I used to, so it's okay. But smoking tonight was sweet. The soup, too, although it was nowhere near my mother's.

Defne is the only person I have long conversations in Turkish with. I talk to my mother and sister on the phone, but our calls last just a few minutes during which I wait for them to be convinced that I'm alive. Sure, there is Ali, but I don't have conversations with him. He only tells me stories until someone cooler than me walks into the changing room. And I don't really listen to him. Then there are the Späti owners, kebab cutters, cashiers of Kreuzberg. But my best interactions with them are limited to exchanges of money and information regarding which city each of us is from. Defne and I have very few things in common: our love for drugs, drinking, and our love-hate for Berlin and Istanbul. She doesn't like to discuss politics, and she claims she never watches Turkish TV. She's not even remotely interested in writing or reading either. But she's one of my best friends here and whenever we get together, we talk a lot. If we don't have anything to speak about, we tell each other the same stories over and again, just to let Turkish words out so we can hear ourselves speak in our mother tongue.

"Ee, daha abi?"

But more often than not, we switch to English without realizing and we can't remember when the switch happened when we try.

"N'olsun ya work, home, work, home."

"Any news from court?"

"Yok."

"Off. Hava da bok gibi zaten. Ben bize bir sigara sarayım en iyisi."

She asked me about the hostel, and I told her about what her archenemy, the head of the maids, is up to, about my shifts with Ali and Mia. I didn't ask her why she didn't tell me this was a cleaning job. For the six months she worked there, she always referred to it as "working at the hostel." When I asked her what she did there exactly, she said she did a bunch of different things, "You know, hostel stuff." I only found out she was a Putzi when I went in for an interview myself.

I don't know if she was ashamed of it or if she really saw the job as simply "working at the hostel." I never confronted her. At the end of the day, it *is* "working at the hostel." We don't have to wear uniforms or put on hairnets. We don't have to call anyone Mr. or Mrs. We're all young and intellectual. We're multikulti. I can't put myself in the same boat as the toilet cleaners at the mall, who are much older, who probably must care for whole families, who are stuck in their jobs. Looking Glass is a stepping-stone for us, right?

But don't we knock on people's doors and say, "Housekeeping"? Don't we get paid minimum wage? Doesn't 10 percent of it go to some extra insurance the hostel makes us pay for so that we're not liabilities? Don't we poison ourselves with their chemicals every day so they can get five-star reviews on Booking.com? Doesn't the head of the maids walk in and out of rooms clapping her hands and yelling, "Come on come on come on! Schnell!"

I asked Defne about her new job, the job that nearly destroyed me. Since it's only been a month, she's still excited about working there. Their teams are separated by languages, so all Turks sit together. When I quit, we were about twenty. When Defne started, there were forty people from Turkey sorting out perverts side by side, day and night. She already befriended all the cool Turks and went on a date with a new guy from the Spanish team. The closest I got to making friends at that job was quietly sharing joints with whoever was offering during cigarette breaks. Then, we'd go back twenty floors up and check posts and profiles that were curated by people from our home countries for us to check.

Female nipples? Check nudity. Beheading? Check terrorism. Woman with short dark hair, innocent face, big breasts, blue jeans holding a newborn baby and asking who wants to fuck them both? Turn off the computer and go out for another cigarette. I smoked so much that I could no longer recognize my voice. I snorted so much coke that I could no longer smell the sting of the city. I danced so much that I could barely stand on my two feet. But I couldn't erase the images and words I saw on the screen. They snuck into my dreams. I saw myself starting fires that killed dozens of people. I saw myself leaving children to drown and die in the Mediterranean. I saw myself killing innocent men and getting away with the crime. Every morning I woke up with an excruciating guilt of being human and an extension of a machine at once. The undeniable and unbearable connection I felt with thousands of profiles I monitored every day.

The company taught us how to clean the filth of humanity from the World Wide Web and in return we fed their artificial intelligence so it could grow tall and get rid of us as soon as possible. Then we all took the long U7 train back to the city with Sternis in our hands, staring at strangers, wondering what secrets they held in their hands as they stared at their phones.

September 1

Today, after work, I got the strongest urge to listen to this Nina Simone song, "Ain't Got No, I Got Life," as if I would collapse then and there on Warschauer Strasse if I didn't. I played it on repeat until I came home.

I've got words, but they don't have freedom. Who has freedom anyway, let alone their words? Not even Germans. I've got no home, I've got no perfume, I've got no faith. I've got no friends, I mean, I do, but most of the time it feels like I don't. So why am I alive anyway? To write? Write what? The kind of book that gets one's family's home raided by the police? A soap to put women to sleep? To clean? To grow old in Turkey, minding my own business, marketing American beauty products to the five people who can afford to buy them? To disappear in a bottle in Berlin?

I'm watching *What Happened, Miss Simone?*

Someone asks Nina Simone: "What's free?"

"It's just a feeling," she says.

"There were times onstage when I really felt free," she says.

"No fear," she says.

Will I ever feel free? I'm always afraid of something. My past, my future, my government, losing my mother, losing my sister, having to move in with my mother and sister, my own body, the dark, the bank, the clock, people, bees. I fear words. I'm afraid of what the world could do to me for putting one word next to the other. I'm afraid of what those words will do to me if I don't. I'm afraid of my genes: alcoholism from my father, depression from my mother, paranoia from one uncle, dementia from another. But I'm more afraid of being normal.

I thought I wouldn't have to pay taxes if I made less than 1,000 euros, but they took it out of my account anyway. I only got paid 240 euros for six days of work, so the next month's pay won't be enough for both rent and health insurance. I hate that money compresses my chest like this. I wish I had a cigarette at least. But there's no way of knowing if I'll have enough money to buy food at the end of the month, so I should stop thinking about cigarettes and start eating less until I find another job.

When I left Istanbul for my new life in Berlin, I'd hoped I'd be getting paid to write by now. Yet here I am, spending the odds and ends of my writing skills to customize and send cover letters to companies that make me sick with their happy hours, stolen names, venomous products, bloodsucking investors, and infectious hypocrisy. They won't even write back with a no, but I must stay positive and fresh and keep looking for that one position hidden somewhere waiting for a worker exactly like me to take, ready to sponsor a visa for me, the most hopeful, grateful, faithful Leyla.

September 7

I've been dreaming about my father coming back to life almost every night for months now. Sometimes as a sick man, sometimes healthier than ever. Some nights he's cheerful, some nights angry and sad, as if he knows it's a dream and he'll have to go back soon. But mostly he's been coming back to save me, to save us. Last night, I was telling him how if only I had 9,000 euros to reapply for a student visa, if only I could start again at another university, I'd do things right this time. I talked to him about drugs and how I'm done. I tried to convince him I haven't gone too far. I told him I never did heroin and how I barely ever did cocaine and even ketamine anymore. *My only vice now is alcohol,* I said to him, *but that shouldn't be a problem for you.* He said, *Leyla, I don't understand why you're being so dramatic. It's only nine thousand euros. Here, take it.* I took the money and felt so light, so safe, so grounded on earth.

September 11

I met Giovanni at Görlitzer Park this morning, where we sat on the steps across the old station and talked about the next show. He wants me to interview an old Italian dancer next, just to have an excuse to meet him. I guess it's fair since I started this whole show to be able to meet Christiane F. She was the first Berlin celebrity I ever knew existed—I was only eleven—and when I first moved to Berlin, I used to tell everyone how reading *Wir Kinder vom Bahnhof Zoo* had changed my life: "Ever since fifth grade, when I first read the book, I knew that I would one day move to Berlin and become a heroin addict." Not all Germans loved the joke, which is probably why I didn't get the first room I viewed when I moved to Berlin.

After I watched the film adaptation while coming down from drugs last year, I could see why. As an adult, all you can see in the movie is children prostituting themselves to old creeps for heroin. And David Bowie. But as a child in Turkey living with depressed and depressing parents, what I felt after reading the book was freedom. Christiane, as a twelve-year-old, could take the train and go to the other end of the city. She met new people every day. She took whatever drug she wanted. She fucked whomever she wanted. People wanted to fuck her. Things happened to her and she did things. Things maybe not always pretty, but certainly exciting. She had mastered the art of escape. Me, I had to wait for years to take that train. Turns out, it stinks. It takes you to work at best, not freedom, and you have to pay.

I told Giovanni that I was trying to find a way to contact Christiane F., when in fact I haven't been trying at all. "Give me another week," I told him as if I were an ambitious producer planning a huge TV show. "If I can't find her, I'll go with your guy."

When I'd set out to find Christiane F. after seeing the movie, I was doing coke or ketamine or both and more at least two or three times a week. How extraordinary I thought my life was. How many hours I spent dancing to the roughest rhythms of Berlin. How much money I wasted. How many sleepless nights I spent, my heart pounding from all the drugs, regretting every line. How easily I forgot all my problems as soon as someone brought me another bag of coke the next night. I wanted to interview Christiane F. because none of the profiles I've read of her questioned whether she loved Berlin or not. I wanted to ask her if she really did not regret never quitting drugs. I wanted to hear her say she's had a fulfilling life after all, even though it cost her a lot. Instead, I kept coming up with excuses for not reaching out. In the beginning, I said I had to prove that the show was worthy of her time, so, as my first guest I invited a performance artist who knew her. The performance artist said that he hadn't seen her since the '90s, but he could introduce me to a DJ I loved. The DJ offered to put me in touch with a band, and somewhere along the way, I stopped thinking about Christiane F. It was easier than admitting that I was terrified of what she might have said. But now, as a cleaner at a party hostel who can't afford any of Berlin's cheap and dirty drugs, as a pair of hands buried in human sweat, hair, shit, and blood, hands attached to a body that feels less mine every day, I need to face Christiane F. more than I ever did before.

A middle-aged German man who'd been sitting near us came to ask for Feuer as I was explaining to Giovanni why Christiane F. was so important to me in less honest words.

"Vielen dank," he said after I handed him my dying lighter. "Go to Hermannplatz on a Tuesday if you want to meet her so much. That's when she gets her methadone prescriptions. She isn't in her best shape though, and I doubt she ever spoke any English."

I walked back home with a familiar embarrassment for being this blind to things that are obvious to everyone else. Why had it never occurred to me before that Christiane F. might not speak English? No wonder there aren't any good stories published about her in English. I imagined cornering her outside her methadone clinic on a Tuesday, trying to convince her to get on a stage with a twentysomething drunk Turk and talk about how Berlin shaped her life, in English. She'd probably tell me to fuck off, if not ignore me altogether. That's what I would do.

Now, I'm listening to Shostakovich's Second Waltz, thinking about Mona and military tanks.

I'm thinking about the night of the attempted coup in Turkey last summer. Mona and I had been high for hours when my mother called and put the phone on speaker so I'd hear the public TV news anchor announce that the military was in charge now. I put my end of the phone call on mute and threw up on the side of Hauptstrasse. (We were on our way to Sisyphos.) I told Mona what was happening, that I had to go home to check the news. We went to her place because it was closer. She settled in her bed and I turned her laptop on. She did more lines while I stayed on the phone with my mother and scrolled through the news updates on Twitter. At one point, I turned around to ask Mona if the French news was covering it, but she had fallen asleep.

My mother said military jets were flying over them, and so did all my friends on the internet. They were scared for their lives even though they were home, but most of them went to sleep eventually. And there I was, high, drunk, shocked in a dirty little room on the thirteenth floor of Mona's high-rise apartment building, watching the sunrise. Fire yellow. Blood orange. Bruise purple. Mediterranean blue. The coup attempt had failed, but so many people died, the whole world saw what happened. (Or did they?) (Who in the West was watching?) I saw the corpses of young men on the old Bosphorus Bridge, the tanks, the bombs. I thought about Ariel Dorfman's "Death and the Maiden." I thought about how my mother's father didn't let her go to college because university campuses were too dangerous after the coup in 1980. I thought about how each military coup sets a country back a hundred years. Or was it fifty? Who said that to me? Was it in history books? Was it a line from a movie? Was it true? What was going to happen to Turkey?

The country has been under what they call a state of emergency since that night. Erdoğan has all the power he needs to do with the country as he pleases. His government already rewrote the constitution, the national school curriculum, and all of our fates. Tens of thousands of people got arrested, were fired from their jobs, or fled to exile. More women get murdered at the hands of men than ever before. Dozens of workers die in workplace accidents every day with no consequences to their employers. Terrorists keep attacking public spaces all around the country, killing fifty to a hundred people at a time.

I've watched it all happen from Berlin. At first, I locked myself in my room. I didn't want to see anyone. I couldn't bring myself to go to a club. There was nothing to celebrate. I didn't know anyone from Turkey in Berlin back then except the Späti owners, who always watched pro-Erdoğan news on TV, or my neighbor who beat her kids every day, calling them a punishment from Allah. My political European friends kept sending me messages like: "It's tragic what's happening to your country. Turkey's going backward instead of forward."

During all this, I only wanted to see Mona. She'd stop by every other week with a bottle of wine, a tube of ketamine, and a bar of Ritter Sport. She'd only ask how I was doing and tell me about the parties she'd been to, the films she'd seen, the books she'd read. Her amphibious appearances and disappearances gave me both a dangerous sense of wholeness and an inexplicable urge to surrender to the loneliness she'd leave me in each time.

Sometimes, she'd be gone for weeks, but she never returned without a new book for me: *Blood and Guts in High School, Bad Behavior, Woman at Point Zero.* She had a bottomless well of films to suggest we watch by a must-know European feminist. She offered each title to me the way one offers a lover a piece of their food in the movies. With every piece of artwork we devoured together, I felt more nationless, ageless, boundless.

If I asked her where she'd been when she was gone, she'd tell me she'd been on vacation with the family of the children she was babysitting or that her dad was visiting—until one very hot Sunday morning at Club der Visionäre, when we were high on a questionable mix of drugs a stranger gave us. I was between jobs and spending money I didn't have. (For some strange reason Sparkasse allowed me to go down to -3,000 euros in overdraft.) (Which they readjusted to -1,000 as soon as I deposited the first 2,000 back.) I told Mona that I wasn't sure whether I was going to go back to Turkey or kill myself when I'd hit the limit. I was only half joking.

"You know you could always find a man to give you money," she said.

"What do you mean?" I asked, my pupils dilated wide, looking back at myself through her eyes.

"That's what I do."

"What?"

"I'm an escort," she said shyly.

And I said, "No you're not!"

The only sex workers I'd been aware of before were those in the profiles I checked at my old job, the back streets of Istanbul, Amsterdam's Red Light District, and of course Christiane F. of Bahnhof Zoo. I couldn't believe Mona could be one of them. She had gone to college. Both her parents were professors. She was the most beautiful, independent, and intelligent friend I had. She liked drugs, yes, but not as much as I did, let alone the children from Bahnhof Zoo. Mona was always in control. I had been a little in love with her since the first time I met her, but she had told me early on she had no interest in either sex or romance after she turned down the first guy who hit on her in the club. How could she have sex for a living then? I had been so oblivious to sex work until that conversation that I didn't know what else to say.

She said, "Think about it" and vanished. Or I was too high to hear her say goodbye. I just remember sitting there alone wondering if I could really do it and how whenever I came close to a decision, a crushing sense of shame took over me. Sex work felt like a stain, like the bleach stain I have on my pants now, that would never go away once I'd let it touch me. Then again, what I found out about Mona didn't change the way I admired her at all. If anything, it made her more compelling to me. Was the shame I felt when I considered doing sex work related to how sex workers are seen in Turkey: worn-out lowlifes whom macho men and boys like those in my high school paid to have sex and bragged about in class? I felt ashamed of how stuck I had been in my Turkish ways of thinking, how backward. And how brave and progressive was Mona, a true feminist!

She didn't respond to my texts for weeks after. Slowly, I stopped thinking about her. I kept applying for more office jobs and tried working on my thesis instead. When we finally met again for drinks at the Späti at Boxi, I apologized for my reaction. She told me not to worry, that it wasn't the first time she got a reaction like that.

"I only told you because you already have sex with a stranger every weekend, you're beautiful, and I don't want you to talk about suicide when we're partying," she said.

"I'm not beautiful," I said, "not like you."

"You are," she said, looking at me as if she were ordering me to think twice.

I obeyed and looked at my reflection in her pupils once again and this time believed her. From that moment on, I never doubted that I was beautiful. I felt terrible many times, like a failure or dirty, but all through it, I've always known I was beautiful, because Mona had said so. She saw me so.

September 14

I was flying again in my dream, lying on an enormous notebook that was also a magic carpet. I was flying across Europe and the Black Sea, as light and happy as one could be.

Then, the notebook started burning. I tried to jump down but couldn't. I woke up but couldn't move my body.

I'd made the mistake of checking the Turkish news again the night before. I fell asleep on the couch while streaming a news channel on my laptop. On the morning news that woke me up, they were still talking about her.

A woman's husband burned her alive while her kids were watching. He was an abusive, gambling, violent drug addict. She had complained to the police eleven times in the last year, but they refused to take any action to protect her. They told her not to be afraid, that he was her husband. He wouldn't really harm her. Any husband could say he would kill his wife when he was angry. It didn't mean that he would actually kill her.

First, he locked the kids in their room. Then, he poured out a bottle of gasoline on his wife. She screamed for help, but no neighbors dared to come between husband and wife. He lit her on fire, got in his car, drove away. She walked after him in flames. The kids watched her burn, fall, and die from their windows.

I have to stop thinking about her. It's not even 10:00 a.m. I have to go to work, knock on tourists' doors, and make sure I sound cheerful when I yell, *Housekeeping!* I still have to live.

Night

All day I thought about fire: the burning, ashes, heat, smell of it. I tried to talk to Ali about it, but he said he didn't want to talk about Turkey. He showed me pictures of the Berghain outfit he wanted to buy when we get paid. A leather collar, handcuffs, and thong set for 150 euros.

Back home, I watched a documentary about Sivas '93, when Sunni Turks burned a hotel where the best writers and poets of Turkey were staying for an Alawite poetry celebration. Thirty-seven people died, burning.

That same year, on my third birthday, four neo-Nazis set fire to the house of a large Turkish family in a German town called Solingen. Five people died—three girls and two women. There are no documentaries about that one. Just a few articles. But Turks in Germany don't need documentaries to learn about neo-Nazis, the attacks in Solingen, Schwandorf, Hoyerswerda, Mölln, or the riot of Rostock-Lichtenhagen. We've all listened to those stories from amcas and teyzes of Kreuzberg in markets, kebab lines, taxi rides. We've always known we were not wanted here, that there are people who despise us so much that they'd burn us alive if they could. But we have Turkish people like that too. And they look like us to boot, talk like us, smell like us. They're indistinguishable from one another and sometimes even ourselves.

It's hard to imagine anything could catch fire in Germany when the streets are wet and cold like tonight, especially when there's so little reference to the fires of the past in public life.

But then again, it's often too easy to forget that the Holocaust took place here, as if the city weren't filled with proof and memorials of its evils. The reminders of one of the most grotesque atrocities of history are our everyday surroundings, those little golden "cobblestones" we step on all the time. Everyone stops noticing them eventually.

In Turkey, it's impossible to forget similar sins because they not only surround us in memoriam but also attack us from every corner, including within ourselves. You're not only never safe but also never not conscious of your unsafety.

When they called, I tried talking to my mother and sister about the woman who died in flames, the tension in the southeast, the academics who lost their jobs for signing a petition for peace. They said I should stop watching the news.

My mother told me about a new soap to watch instead. My mother who used to tell me all husbands beat their wives and kids when they drank. All husbands drank and cheated. My mother who used to tell me not to tell anyone about the monster my father turned into at night because we were family, and our monster loved his family more than any other father. My mother who read all the novels she got her hands on, watched all the movies, documentaries, and soaps she could to escape her reality. My mother taught me how to do the same.

"Bu dizinin oyuncuları çok iyi," she said. So, I'm drinking my free beer and waiting for the soap to load. Two more sips and no more news and everything is going to be alright.

I'm still here. I live here. I'm here.

September 17

I met Aria at the lake after work yesterday. She's the only writer left in my life. All the other writers I knew went back to their home countries after spending a couple winters reading the same pieces in bar basements over and again or got startup jobs and stopped writing. Aria stayed and kept working on her novels. She has two manuscripts already at the age of thirty, though neither of them have been published. She used to write every day, but the rejections seem to be getting to her. These days all she does is hang out with her boyfriend's friends and swim in Berlin's filthy lakes. I've never swum in a lake here. It feels like I'd be cheating on the Mediterranean—and for what? The water always looks grimy, just like everything else in this city. I like sitting on grass and watching people descend into the lake though. It calms me down.

It was as hot as an August day and all of Berlin had gathered by the lake, topless and drunk. The sun shone on us like we were in Agnès Varda's *Le Bonheur*, except with people's pastel outfits replaced by bare skin, cheap beers, and tobacco in their hands instead of flowers. Aria and I found a little pocket of shade under a tree to write and read in peace, but of course we also got drunk and took our tops off before too long. As it often does when we are alone together, the conversation came around to her Jewish upbringing in New York and my Americanized childhood in Turkey.

I told Aria how in primary school, I thought there were a couple of women covered in black sheets in each city. And I was sure that those women in black were evil, out to get us little girls and cover our hair too. So, whenever we saw such women on the streets while riding the school bus, together with a couple of other kids, I stuck my head out of the high rectangular windows and yelled, *BOO! BOO! BOO!* Or maybe this only happened once. I don't trust my memory, but it replays this one scene so vividly. I remember the terrified look in the eyes of one woman. She must have been younger than I am now.

Aria told me about her mother and three sisters who all wear wigs to cover their hair. She was sure that non-Jewish passersby were making fun of her family, but they lived in such a mighty bubble that they didn't see the non-Jewish people around them. She grew up in an all-Jewish neighborhood, went to a Jewish school, a Jewish college, and then to Israel, where she lived with dozens of other Jewish girls trying to learn how to be better Jews.

I was about to make a comment on perception and awareness and bubbles, but Aria said in a low voice, "Hey. Look at that guy over there. Is he doing what I think he's doing?"

Behind the bushes sat a skinny and pale German around our age, butt naked. His eyes were fixed on us and his hand was on his dick. He sat with his legs crossed like he was meditating, only he was masturbating. I started laughing. The setting sun made his white skinny legs look lake green. He looked like a giant grasshopper. Aria wasn't laughing at all.

"Stop it!" she shouted.

He smiled and moved his hand up and down his dick so violently I couldn't keep myself from looking. I thought he was trying to hurt himself.

"You're disgusting," Aria yelled as we walked past him with as much distance as possible.

He said, "Thank you." And he meant it. He probably came right after we left.

On the U-Bahn, Aria couldn't stop talking about how Berlin's sexual liberation had gone too far. How he had no right to make us part of his sexual experiment without our consent. I agreed with her, even though my first reaction was different. I had thought it was funny. It was Berlin. And it's not like he tried to touch us or come too close. But he did pull us into his sexual fantasies and did not let us go after Aria asked him to. When I caught the irritated eyes of an older German lady watching us as we spoke on the train, I realized how hot the masturbator must have thought it was to objectify us like that. A Turk and an American, a Muslim and a Jew at his majesty's service.

We bought another bottle of wine and chips and came to my apartment. Victor was at home with a new German guy he found on some app. The German, Markus, sat where I usually do in the kitchen. He had his legs crossed as well. His bare toes were looking at me as if to say, *Who are you? This is our home now.*

Victor was making tacos. The kitchen was a mess. Whenever Victor cooks, the kitchen looks like a war zone: oil, dirty dishes, paper towels everywhere, onion skins, tomato juice, pickles. I hate pickles. (But what's more horrifying than pickles is the fact that I'm writing all these words in my diary.) (Head of the maids, you need to get out of my head—or is this you, Mother?)

Aria told them what happened.

"Was he a refugee?" Markus asked. "I hear a lot of stories of homeless refugees harassing people these days."

I said, "He looked as German as you," took the wine bottle and two glasses, and walked into my room. Aria closed the door after us. We exchanged one look and opened our wine.

Aria's grandparents fled Berlin during World War II and moved to New York as refugees. Both of her parents grew up hearing Holocaust stories from their parents. When they found each other, Aria imagines, they must have been desperate to get out of their family homes faded by grief. They got married when they were barely eighteen and had five children in five years. Aria was the youngest one in her family, like me. She was the only one to question the strict rules that defined her life, where she would go, who she could see, like me. Her parents thought spending a year studying the Torah in Israel would recenter Aria. Shipping problem kids off to Israel worked for most American Jewish families, but it was not going to work for Aria. After a few months in the Torah school, she moved to Berlin. Fast-forward a decade, Aria is friends with all sorts of godless sinners and in love with a goy from Australia.

But the rules she was forced to memorize while growing up still persecute a huge part of her life. She's afraid of her parents finding out that Paul is not Jewish before she convinces him to convert. Paul, who is an atheist, is not vehemently against the idea. It's not like he'll be betraying another religion by "converting" to Judaism to make life easier for Aria. But in return, he wants Aria to promise that she won't raise their kids as believers. Aria can't make that promise.

"Could you imagine not getting your children circumcised?" she asked me last night.

"Well, yeah, and not only because I will never have children," I said. "But also because it's inhumane to cut people's body parts off without their consent."

"For sure," she said. "But if my kids aren't Jewish, my family will never truly accept them. How can I deprive my mother of her grandchildren and my children of their grandmother, the woman who raised me, who dedicated her whole life to care for her family?"

Aria and I understand each other. That's why we were drawn to each other the first night we met at a spoken-word event where we both read stories about our mothers, when everyone else read poems about being young and free. Our perspectives on life might be different, but we are similar in our relationship with our families. Both of our mothers gave their kids all they had. And even though we never asked for it, it's our turn to give back.

Aria needs to give her mother good Jewish grandkids, and I have to find a way to make enough money to take care of my mother as soon as possible. I have to pick up the phone whenever she calls, no matter how tired I feel from working all day to try and make this happen. And I have to make sure I don't sound too stressed out on the phone so she won't die on me too.

Most people don't understand why I feel responsible for my mother. "You don't owe her anything," they say. But not Aria.

How could we deprive them of the daughters they raised to become their allies, their cellmates in the prison called life, because we want to not only have but also to show off having the freedom and happiness that they never did?

Treasures of the day:

A big bottle of Gordon's (I found two bottles of rosé and swapped them with Mia who found the gin cleaning the second floor.)

Blue sweatpants, just my size (I'll start wearing them to work.)

2 cents

5 euros' worth of Pfand

A copy of *My Brilliant Friend* by Elena Ferrante

Eve couldn't stop bringing up *My Brilliant Friend* on the show last month, so I read the first few pages in the room where I found it. I tried to like it because Aria loves Elena Ferrante too. But I don't think I can. I can't read about childhood because I can't bear thinking about my own. I don't have any happy memories from my childhood. A bitter taste is attached to every photograph that comes to my mind. Maybe I could have felt differently if anyone in my extended family had children. If I could replace child Leyla's fears with their smiles. But all the women in my family are either single without children or widows, and all of my grandparents died before I was born, except one. My father's mother lived until I was five, but her whole body was paralyzed. Even from her wheelchair, she terrorized the room with her blue eyes, telling everyone what they could and couldn't do. I wasn't allowed to play games around her, or else she would pierce my skin with her flaming eyes and groan, as if it were a crime for me to move. So I'm not a fan of Elena narrating her life as an older woman either.

I left the book in the lost and found. I wish I could leave these uninvited memories in a basket too.

I invested my Pfand money in tonic and lime because Victor loves his gin and tonic. But of course he's not home. He must be working late again.

When Victor and I first met, we were inseparable, student-workers at the same startup. Victor was on the tech team, I in marketing. I'd been living in Berlin for a year. Victor had moved from Havana just a week before. It was his first time outside Cuba, and everything fascinated him: the grocery stores, the U-Bahn, the office, the streets, their newness. I knew the feeling. He had this untamed energy and will to work for hours, dance on the streets, make friends with strangers, tell stories, go on dates, then make it to all his classes. He was the one who saved me from my loneliness when I was ready to give up on making real friends in Berlin. He lured me out to bars and spontaneous trips. He taught me German and Spanish words with the determined compassion of my mother when she used to try to feed little me broccoli. Three months after we met, we decided to move in together.

61

We've spent countless nights together in this apartment telling each other about our lives. Victor told me so much about his happy family of three in Havana that I felt like I knew them, like a child knows and embraces families in movies as her own. Victor's parents worked for the state: one as a bus driver, the other as a porter. His grandparents who took care of him when his parents were at work are still alive and well.

Victor studied software engineering and after graduation started working for the state himself for 15 euros a month. That's how much a state worker made in Cuba. But money wasn't the reason he wanted to get out. And it wasn't the fact that he was gay and coming out to his family was never going to be an option. He wanted to leave because to him Cuba was a prison, a happy prison where all inmates danced salsa and drank Cuba libre under the sun but a prison nevertheless.

Cuban TV had only ever shown one channel—filled with government propaganda. Around the time Victor started college, an anonymous group came up with an alternative to the practically nonexistent internet and TV broadcast: distributing external hard drives with recent episodes of foreign TV series, soap operas, music, and films every morning to every corner of the island. They called it El Paquete. At first, Victor loved El Paquete. But then the sneak peek at what the world had to offer made him angry. As a software engineering student, Victor had joined the lucky few to have access to the internet, but he could only use it for academic or professional reasons. What difference did he have from the prisoners in Guantánamo, if he was not even allowed to watch the shows he wanted, let alone earn enough money to travel outside the island?

When Victor was in college, his professor offered him a job as an off-the-record freelancer for a German tech company, building artificial intelligence systems. He would make 100 euros a month after his professor took his cut for *graciously* taking care of the logistics so Victor wouldn't need to worry about getting caught. The professor would put himself at risk to receive the paycheck, exchange the currency, and pay Victor at the end of each month. Victor knew the rules of the game. A year later, shortly after meeting the Germans themselves on Skype for the first time, he started working for them directly but of course secretly. Then, he was making 250 euros a month for over forty hours of work per week.

His team manager kept telling him he was their best developer, but whenever Victor tried to talk to him about moving to Europe, he said the company couldn't afford to sponsor a visa. This was also part of the game Victor knew, for if Victor lived in Germany, they would have to pay him at least twenty times more. It took Victor four years to save up enough money to move to Germany with a student visa. In the meantime, he graduated from college and completed his mandatory military service, while living with his family and dancing by the Caribbean every night.

He moved to Berlin without knowing anyone except his online colleagues from the tech company who no longer wanted to work with him, but it took him only a few days to find the job at the startup where we met, as student-workers. He made over 1,000 euros now for twenty hours per week and felt like the luckiest man on earth.

Whenever I complained about work, he'd say, "Would you rather be unemployed in Turkey?"

Whenever I complained about the coldness of Berliners, he'd say, "I'd take a cold German over a butt-in Caribbean or Mediterranean any day."

At the end of his first year, he was only dating cold Germans, always wearing black Berlin clothes, and had stopped dancing salsa. Then, he started working full-time and stopped going out at night. Instead, he bought a new kitchen for our apartment and all the robots he could: three Alexas, three different cooking robots, a Roomba that vacuums, mops, and shines. He changed the door lock to a coded one and installed an alarm. He signed up for all delivery services: Amazon, Rewe, Delivery Hero. Buying, owning, using became the only things that got him excited.

People who've met us in the last year or two always ask how we ended up friends. What could two opposite characters like us have in common? How can I live in an apartment like this when all I ever talk about is how much I despise capitalism? Does Victor even talk? He does. We talk.

We have a language of our own. A language of few words. We owe it to El Paquete, which always included the latest episodes of the most popular Turkish soaps, dubbed in Spanish. "Amor prohibido" were the first words he said to me when he found out I was from Turkey. I pretended to understand what he was saying (as I mostly do when people speak to me in languages I'm not fluent in), but he kept exclaiming Spanish titles of soaps from Turkey until I got him: "*Amor prohibido! Las mil y una noches! El sultán!*" And our language of few words was born. It grew as we watched and rewatched all those soaps together with English subtitles, binging through whole seasons in one night, as if we could rewrite the years we first watched them as teenagers.

He's too busy to watch anything with me now, but he still asks me about my visa, my case, my work, my friends, my family back home. He doesn't ask about my writing, okay, but also never interrogates me about what I'm planning to do with my future if I can't figure out a way to stay. He trusts that I will. And I don't lecture him about capitalism like the so-called communist Westerners who have access to everything. I know what he's been through to break free and make it here. He knows I won't go back, because I can't.

I am his witness as he is mine, that this place is home to us both, that we're no longer surrounded by wired walls, and we never will be again.

But who'll believe me when I say this is my home if my witness is never home anymore?

September 23

I haven't worked a shift in five days. I kind of miss it.

September 24

Mohamed has been texting me every weekend since Sisyphos, and since none of my friends wanted to hang out last night, I invited him over. He came with half a bottle of gin and a pink minidress for me. It was too small. He said he got it for me at Humana, but I suspect he found it on the street walking to my place. He also gave me two pills, even though I told him I didn't like pills. "You can trade them for lines next time you go clubbing," he said. He poured us gins without tonics as I watched him move his body in my home as if he's always lived here with me. No, as if neither of us lived here and we had both snuck into a stranger's apartment to play house.

I think most of what he told me were lies. I didn't mind. He didn't seem to remember much about me except my nationality and the size of my ass since he kept referring to and touching my Turkish booty while he talked. I didn't mind that either. He told me about his family in Liberia and that he lost his mother and two brothers when he was a little boy. I asked how but instead of answering me, he asked where Heidi was. Can't say I wasn't slightly annoyed. After we had sex the last time, he kept telling me things like, "I love your ass. I'm glad we didn't end up having sex with Heidi. German girls are like sticks. They're

too cold, they don't know how to move." But he clearly
still wanted to fuck Heidi.

Then, he told me about his hustle in Berlin—the huge
and cheap apartment he lives in with his cool German
roommate and how he gets unemployment benefits from
the Jobcenter and works at a bar under the table.

"But you can't extend your visa if you apply for unemployment!" I said, scandalized.

"Why on earth would I want to stay in Germany?" he
asked. "I'll be out of here as soon as I'm done with school."

I envied his carelessness, how casual his feelings for
Berlin were. And he had three years on his student visa! I
drank all the gin in my glass in one gulp and then another,
waiting for Mohamed to either ask me a question or take
me to bed. But he was too excited. He wanted to tell me
about the IT program he came here to attend and his plans
to set up an IT firm in his hometown. I had to drag him
to the bedroom myself.

Interesting how Mohamed has so many opinions about
how monotone Germans are in bed when he can only have
orgasms strictly doing missionary while I twist his nipples
for an hour. Okay, it's probably more like half an hour.
Maybe just ten minutes. But it sure feels like an hour. The
first night, when Heidi left us alone in my room, when we
got under my duvet and I was still high, it was fun. I told
him to do the same to me. I nodded when he gestured
toward choking me and pulling my hair. I said yes when
he asked me, while he was inside me, if I wanted to have a
threesome with him and a friend of his who had a bigger

cock than him. Last night, I fell asleep while my fingertips were holding his nipples and he was inside me.

Before he left, Mohamed said he wanted to book a room at the hostel and wait for me naked until it's my time to clean his room. Is this the most messed up fantasy in the world, or is he the only honest man around me to share his first thoughts when he hears the word "cleaner"?

Pinching Mohamed's nipples until he comes in a bunk bed at Looking Glass would have to be the final scene of my life if it were a movie. No. It would be too sad a scene for any director to make me play, even if my life were a soap opera.

September 26

Last night in my dream, I was walking to Giovanni's Room to tell Giovanni that I'd finally convinced Christiane F. to be a guest on the show. I kept falling, my pantyhose tore, my knees bled and hurt, but I kept walking with the thrill of the news I wanted to give. When I finally arrived at the entrance of the theater, I heard Mia from work, Giovanni, and his crush talking and laughing in Italian. When they realized I was there, they laughed even harder and louder. They didn't have to tell me. I knew that Mia was replacing me as the host of the show. I left quietly. On the walk back home, in front of a shop's glass window, I saw myself in my cleaning outfit, sweaty and wrinkled.

I woke up, drank a cup of cold black coffee Heidi left on the table, and walked to the theater. I rang Giovanni's doorbell for as long as it took him to come through.

"I can't do another event until I find Christiane F. You'll have to find someone else to host it if you want to have other guests," I said.

"Are you okay, darling?" he asked.

"I'm great!" I said. "It's a Tuesday."

I hugged him goodbye and walked to Hasenheide. I didn't want to stop for the U-Bahn. I was going to find Christiane and convince her to do the event. I was going to come home and start writing a story about a girl trying to stay in Berlin. I was going to cut my hair, clean my room, read a Virginia Woolf novel.

It started to rain the moment I arrived at the clinic's gates. I had my dress on and nothing to cover my head with. An angry old man pushed me to the right. I think he said something like, "Are you going in oder was?"

Of course I was never going to go in there. How did I ever think that I could? What could I possibly tell Christiane if I found her? And in German!

I got back underground to the U8 and returned to my bed.

September 27

I found 6 cents but lost 13 euros today on a taxi I took to the wrong address with my trash bag full of Pfand bottles. I was trying to make it to a meeting with an immigration lawyer who is a friend of a friend of Heidi's, to which I didn't even want to go. I know all my options already, but I didn't want to seem ungrateful, and I didn't want Heidi to think I wasn't doing everything I could.

The Turkish radio in the taxi was reporting on the Iraqi Kurdish independence referendum and how no one was going to acknowledge the results.

"Kodumun teröristleri," the driver said.

I asked him what was so wrong about wanting independence. He looked at me from the rear mirror and asked if I was one of those PKK sympathizers.

I'm not. I don't have the luxury of ignorance to support militants while living comfortably in my Western country of citizenship. Any of my friends, ex-boyfriends, unrequited love interests from high school, cousins, neighbors could end up in the battlefield during their mandatory military service and have to decide whether to die or become a killer at once. You could be an apolitical Kurdish boy from Izmir who went to school for fashion design and you could find yourself in the same place. I can't romanticize the PKK, I won't romanticize martyrdom in battlefields, and I don't romanticize teenagers dying to preserve death pools that put billions of euros in the pockets of so-called Western civilization. My Western friends accuse me of secret nationalism because I insist the PKK doesn't represent all Kurds. Yet my country's laws could persecute me for saying the Turkish military doesn't represent all Turks.

Once, Heidi had brought home a PKK flag to hang out our kitchen window. A photograph of Apo was printed on the flag, too, the one where he's holding a white dove with one hand and an AK-47 with the other, smiling. When I said it made me uneasy, she said, "But the Kurds need the PKK to stand up for their rights, whether we approve of all their actions or not."

"How can you know that?" I had asked her. "Have you ever held a gun?" And then, "Do you think Middle Easterners inherently crave battles? Do you think being ruled by dictators and fighting each other on mountains is in our DNA? Do you think no Turk, Kurd, or Arab would rather organize poetry readings, have long philosophical discussions, Sunday meals with their families, or dance with friends? Our deaths are not video games where you can earn bonus points by clicking on the 'root for the victim' button. Do you think it's only the Western countries who deserve to decide the fates of their nationhood with democracy?"

I was reliving this conversation, which had made the limitations of our friendship impossible to unsee, and thinking about how this referendum will cause even more unrest in the region. All dictators will unite against Kurds, and the West will stay silent again when it comes to diplomacy. They will keep shaking hands with dictators on TV and rub their hands in secret meetings thinking about all the new guns they can sell now, all the new oil they can claim by an intervention. Why else would they let this referendum happen? Yes, it all sounds premeditated. Or is it my mistrustful Turkish mind that sees everything as rehearsed tragedies now, every catastrophe as an inside job, bound to play itself out no matter what the little people want?

The radio was now reporting on America's expanded travel ban and how Trump claimed it would protect the US from terrorists. The driver was looking at me through the mirror as if I had committed the ultimate sin by asking what was so wrong with a referendum for independence. Before I could answer his question, I realized we were going to the wrong side of the city. Turns out, there are two Waldstrasses in Berlin. I got out of the car thirty minutes away from home. I walked to the closest Rewe, returned my bottles, got on a bus, and came back to my bed.

My sister's calling.

I don't want to talk to anyone. And maybe I don't want to be here. But if not here, where?

September 30

Aria came over today to write together but we spent most of our time making hummus, drinking wine, and complaining about the literary world.

"Berlin's poetry scene sucks."

"The publishing world is just a couple of rich people pretending to enjoy reading."

"You're the best poet in Berlin."

"We were born into the wrong century."

We both received rejection emails today from the Berlin emerging writer grant we had applied for in June. I'd sent them a short story about Shahmaran and three poems: one about worker bees, one about murdered activists, and one about my mother's TV. I wrote a letter in which I made up a plot for a novel I'd write with the grant about three immigrants in Berlin: a thief, a doctor, and a housewife. I didn't have high hopes of winning the grant, nor did I ever feel compelled to start this novel since I applied, but I daydreamed about it every now and then. How I would drop my case against the university and let them know I didn't need their mercy, quit my job, renew my visa. And what I'd do with the 2,500 euros the grant would pay me each month for a whole year! But they gave it to a journal-published, MFA-holding, successfully employed American man instead.

"Didn't he get enough chances in life to *emerge* already?" I asked Aria.

"How are we supposed to get anywhere if the only ones who win grants are those who have won other grants before?"

We made a bet on what his book was going to be about. Aria thinks it will be about an affair between a young girl and a tormented, emotionally unavailable man. I think it will be about the struggles of being a white American abroad. Whoever loses will buy the other five bottles of wine. If we both win, we will get drunk and sabotage all his book readings in Berlin. If we both lose, we will send him a bottle.

If I'll still be around, of course. But we didn't mention this last part.

October 3

Today I ran into Eve on the U-Bahn. I thought she'd gone back to Poland after the show, but it turns out she met a handsome German in the audience that night and after spending the next two days with him, decided to stay in Berlin. She'd been living with the German since then, but a few days ago she finally moved into her own place.

"I tried to message you, but you disappeared from my Friends lists on Facebook and Instagram after the event. I thought you blocked me," she said.

I told her I deleted all my accounts and asked if she wanted to come over for a drink.

"You read my mind," Eve said.

"Just promise me one thing," I said. "You'll never take a photo of me when we're together. You'll never post about me. I want to be untraceable. I want the internet to forget that I ever existed."

She promised. At first, she looked like she was going to ask why, but she didn't.

Eve bought us a bottle of wine from the Späti (I told her I had two bottles of beer in my bag, but she said she doesn't drink beer) and told me about Stefan, her new apartment, how she felt like she never left Berlin and has known Stefan all her life.

She asked if I had updates on my case. I said no. She asked if I had any updates on my love life. I said no. (Not unless I count Mohamed, who only sent me selfies without any words attached to them since we last met, in a bathroom with a mirror full of stains.) (I didn't text him back. What could I have said?)

I guess she felt bad about the good news she shoved in my face and started telling me how she's been getting paid less and less for Instagram posts, how little money she has in her savings account, and how Stefan was kind of sexist.

"You don't need to hide your happiness, Eve," I said. "It's not your fault I failed my thesis and I don't even want a boyfriend."

"No, I mean it," she said. "And he's weird in bed."

"What do you mean?" I asked.

She said, "Never mind."

But when Stefan texted Eve to meet him at a bar in Mitte shortly after her confessions, her smile came back, her face glowed, and she refreshed her makeup in the bathroom while singing a Polish song. I sat on the side of the bathtub with my wine. Watching her get ready, I thought about texting Mohamed, but I decided not to.

October 5

Cleaning products give me a special kind of a headache: piercing through all music and daydreaming I try to blanket my brain under, they burn it with their chemicals.

Turkish soaps are on a five-week break because of the economic crisis. My mother told me this. She was pretty sad. But I think it will be good for her, me, and the whole country to take a little break.

What do I do with my time after work without blowing up my aching head?

Treasures of the day:

A bottle half-full of Baileys

Bio milk (the good stuff) (which I am drinking as I write these lines)

My Brilliant Friend (No one claimed it so I thought I may as well bring it home.)

October 8

I didn't have work today. I woke up without the alarm. The coffee was warm. Heidi and Victor weren't home. I told Victor's Roomba to clean the apartment and sat on the couch in the kitchen, staring at the ceiling until my mother and sister called. I finally told them about my job. They took it unexpectedly well, which only made me feel worse about failing in Berlin after I abandoned them when they needed me to mourn my father's death and heal together.

They did tell me to return to Turkey if things were too hard but didn't insist. They also know that if I go back to Turkey once, there's no way of getting out again anytime soon. Back in Turkey I would have two options: go live on my aunt's old couch in that tiny apartment in the middle of nowhere, where my mother and sister have been staying since last year because they can't afford to pay rent *and* my father's debts off at the same time. My aunt told them they could stay with her up to two years and finds a way to remind them of her generosity every day they say.

I could also crash on friends' expensive couches in Istanbul until each of them gets sick of me or until I find a job for barely above minimum wage. My whole salary would have to be spent on rent and food, and if I ever won the appeal in Berlin, I simply wouldn't have the money to come back here again. I couldn't show the Ausländerbehörde enough money in my account to extend my visa. One euro is worth almost 5 Turkish liras today, which makes the monthly minimum wage of a full-time job there only a couple hundred euros.

My sister makes minimum wage and half of it goes to feed both her and my mother. She's been trying to save the other half for a deposit and a couple months' rent for a new apartment, but whenever she comes close to it, an urgent need sweeps all of it away. My mother doesn't have access to her retirement income because she was a partner in my father's firm on paper and now has to pay back all the loans he took before he died. They haven't even been able to visit me in Berlin. It's impossible to get out of Turkey now unless you are very, very lucky. I had luck once. A lot. And I wasted it all.

October 9

Berlin is dark again. It's cold, quiet. It's my favorite time of the year. Before I moved to Berlin, I only visited the city in winter. When I finally moved here it was already fall, which quickly turned into winter. People would ask why I loved Berlin so much when I'd only experienced its worst. They would argue there wasn't anything to like about the city in the cold. Everyone stayed inside. There were no festivals, no dancing outside, no picnics in parks. There was only the dark sky, which occupied the city at 3:00 p.m. and stayed until morning, driving young boys and girls to suicide, destitute adults into addiction.

I wouldn't tell them that I'd come from the Mediterranean where the sun occupies cities and takes lives as she pleases without being bothered to hide her cruelty in her shadows or snow, where all adults I knew were lonely addicts and the young people were too busy trying to survive to kill themselves.

I'm staying in a friend's apartment who's away for work and renting out my own room on Airbnb. I charge 50 euros per night for four nights. So it's almost worth sharing Ash's apartment with his sixty-year-old German roommate who keeps speaking to me in German even though I tell him, "Ich kann nicht sprechen auf Deutsch," which explains how he and Ash get along so well. Ash is the kind of friend who keeps talking to you while you're trying to focus on something else, and when you tell him you can't concentrate, he says, "Just ignore me, I'm talking shite" and keeps telling you about his dates, work drama, and weekly weed review.

I haven't seen Ash since the summer. We text every now and then, but I'm pretty sure he's avoiding meeting me because I'm too depressed. But he never promised to be a bad-weather friend. He's always been afraid of getting too close to sadness. I can understand that.

Ash found this room through a dodgy craigslist ad years ago, but it's my first time coming here. It's always Ash who comes over and sleeps on my couch. He's a Ryanair flight attendant, so he wants to be close to the airport. But he hates not being in the center of action, so he spends most nights in Berlin on other people's couches, strangers' beds, or in clubs. I never thought I'd have a reason to take the train all the way to Spandau, but here I am. This is a five-bedroom apartment, but all rooms except the old man's and Ash's are locked. Their kitchen is old, tiny, and dark; their huge dining room, with floral wallpaper and a beautiful Virgin Mary painting hanging on the wall, feels like it belongs to another apartment, another century, a family.

When the roommate is at work, I like to sit here at their mid-century cherry dining table and think about what could be hidden inside all the locked rooms. Books? Furniture and clothes that once belonged to happy children who died in a terrible accident? Maybe someone killed herself here. Or maybe she killed her husband. I've been here for two days, but it feels like it's been weeks since I left Kreuzberg and moved into this quiet old-time dimension. I only walk back and forth in the hallway, as if I were locked in here. I'm not. I could get out and walk down the stairs and then to a park, but I don't want to.

The house I grew up in had a room that was always locked. It also had five rooms. My room, with the balcony where my mother used to hang out the laundry to dry; my sister's room, which I took over after she left for college; my mother's room, where I slept most nights; the sitting room, where my father watched TV, drank raki, and slept every night; the guest room, where no one has ever slept, since we never had any guests. Then there was the big salon with its closed doors, where my mother disappeared to once every hour making the door creak like a cuckoo clock—which I always wanted to have as a child, but my mother told me it only existed in the movies. She would say salons were for special guests, and since there was not a single special soul in our godforsaken city, our salon was for no one but her.

For the longest time I thought my mother did something secret, dangerous, or supernatural in that room no one else went into. Not even my father. One summer, the earth shook Turkey with serial earthquakes and killed thousands of people throughout the country. Those of us who survived drove our cars to open fields to spend the night away from the cheap buildings our ancestors had planted on our cursed land. When we returned home, my mother ran straight to her salon. I heard her cry and let myself in through the open door after her. I found her sitting on the floor in tears, trying to put together her tea set. Cracked, split, and shattered vases, frames, and ashtrays were all over the floor.

A few years later, I discovered that my mother was going in there to smoke. I immediately knew that I had to smoke too. I was to do everything my mother did without question. I was her daughter. I was her. Her touch felt like my own. Anything she gave me, I devoured. I looked like her too. I still do. In the old Turkish movies we watched together on her TV, the main woman's daughter would always grow up to look exactly like her mother. The actress would then start playing two roles. She would have gray hair and wrinkles when she played the mother, and she wore modern, colorful clothes when she played the daughter. My sister was always my father's daughter and I was my mother's. Until I wasn't. Until I realized why my mother didn't like the company of others. She didn't want witnesses, because she must have known that all families weren't like ours even though she kept saying so to herself and to us. If she really thought they were, why would she mind what others thought of her life at home? She didn't want any spectators to see how her husband's eyes flamed with anger when she did the wrong thing, how his impending beating could be felt in the alcohol-infused air before it landed on her lips, my hair, my sister's back.

So I set out to make a life for myself that would be the exact opposite of hers. I surrounded myself with people to make sure there would always be someone who wanted to come over to my apartment. I made lounges out of every room I lived in, where I turned strangers into friends, friends into witnesses.

But why does it feel like it's me crying there now, sitting on the floor of the salon in our old house, perpetually trying to put together broken pieces?

October 11

I'm on the U-Bahn back to Kreuzberg. Before I left the apartment after my four-day stay, Ash's roommate gave me a book by Thomas Mann: *Der Tod in Venedig*. I tried to tell him I couldn't read German, but he didn't want to hear it. He said I had to learn German now that I had a book to read. (I think.)

Evening

When I got home, I found a yellow envelope in the mailbox, sent to me from the German court. This faded old-world yellow means that I have to respond within two weeks. The university's law department informed the court that they would not be changing their decision to fail me and my thesis. At least this is what I glean from Google's image translator.

This either means that court specialists will reevaluate my thesis or there'll be a hearing soon, but *soon* in German standards—so I'll still have to apply for an extension on my Fiktionsbescheinigung. I need to ask Heidi to help me understand what the letter says exactly, but I'm relieved she's not home today. I don't have the strength. I haven't even changed the bedsheets yet.

When we first moved into this apartment, we'd all Airbnb our rooms frequently. We'd take trips or go clubbing with the money, or we'd sleep in each other's rooms to spend less on rent. It was fun to tidy up after guests when the money was just a reward. Victor and Heidi grew out of it when they started earning more at work, and it felt odd to be the only one bringing strangers into our space, so I stopped too. They didn't mind that I did it now, knowing how little I make and how much I could use the money, but I didn't realize how alienating it would feel to come back to my room, the only thing that's mine, and to have to clean it as if it were a room at the Looking Glass.

October 13

I finally ran into Heidi in the apartment and asked for her help reading and responding to the court letter. I was right. The university is not willing to give me another chance. We wrote that I would not be changing my mind about appealing and requested an outsider's evaluation or a hearing. After we finished writing the letter, I gave Heidi a thank-you beer and cooked us dinner. Then, we watched a film called *This Is Not a Film* by Jafar Panahi.

When the Iranian government bans Panahi from directing films and puts him under house arrest in Tehran, he invites a friend over and asks him to follow him with a camera. Panahi starts reading the script he wrote in hopes of directing. It's about a girl who wins the university exams, but her family locks her inside the house so she can't enroll.

Panahi quickly gets frustrated with the impossibility of making a movie by reading the script. He talks about how while shooting one of his past movies, a child actor decided she didn't want to stay still and play the role of the girl on the bus. He shows us, using the TV screen in his own apartment, the scene in which the little girl asks the men to stop the bus, gets out, starts yelling, telling people she doesn't want to get back on the bus. We hear Panahi's voice in the background. He tells his camera crew to keep shooting. He explains to his friend holding the camera, to us, that these unexpected acts make a movie what it is.

Then a young man comes to collect the trash. Panahi asks him who he is. He says he's the janitor's brother-in-law. He says he's been in Mr. Panahi's building many times before, he's seen him, collected his trash. Panahi doesn't remember the young trashman but decides to get in the elevator and keep recording. The trashman says he shouldn't, that it stinks inside the elevator, that he has to stop on each floor and ring all the bells and collect everybody's trash. Panahi is already in, asking if he's also a janitor.

He says he's doing a master's in art history. Or something like it at least, according to the English subtitles.

When the elevator reaches the basement, the student-trashman leaves the building to put the trash out. Panahi wants to follow him. There are a lot of men outside and fireworks.

"Mr. Panahi, please don't come outside," he says. "They'll see you with the camera."

Panahi stays inside the building.

The film comes out and wins all the awards.

Watching the end credits, I sat still and grieved the distance and difference between us—Panahi, a middle-aged Iranian director who is on house arrest, unable to direct the movie he wrote about a young girl who is on house arrest, and me, a Turkish runaway in her twenties who came to Berlin to be free but can't bring herself to write a book that would expose the world for what it is.

Then, Heidi asked if I knew any political Turkish films like this one.

I said I didn't. Not that I could think of. Nothing contemporary at least. I had been avoiding my own country's art as if I could ever separate myself from the pain, guilt, rage we're all doomed to carry no matter where we go, rage we are not even allowed to scream about, make films about, write about, sing about. The rage in my paralyzed grandmother's eyes, the pain in my mother's eyes when she talks of her youth terrorized by my grandmother and her son, my father. And the guilt I inherited and carried with me all the way here, the guilt that I try to numb by drinking.

I surrendered to drugs, sabotaged my education, distanced myself from everyone who loved me after only twenty-four years in the world. One summer of protesting in Istanbul and one failed military coup attempt that I followed online from my new home in another country tipped me over the edge. My father and mother stayed in Turkey through two military coups, six decades of political chaos, corruption, conflict. They lived through abuse, poverty, lovelessness. But then again. One of them is gone, and the other can barely leave the apartment anymore. All she wants to do is cook, clean, and watch soaps. And all I want to do is to shout, scream, howl when I'm with her. *Wake up, mother, wake up, he's gone now*, I want to say. And I did, too, many times. But it only made her angry, then quiet, then sad. She always had the same answer: "Benden geçti artık."

Even if my father is dead, even if all fathers like mine were dead, the president is still alive. And even if this president would die, another one of the same kind would rise to power. There's always a mustache lurking in a corner, waiting to threaten us, hit us, take us. There'll always be more of them than us.

I'm jealous of how Heidi can appreciate the beauty of our culture without feeling the pain. Without feeling claustrophobic in a projection. Without remembering her own frustrations as a little girl growing up in cities that look like Tehran, sound like Tehran, hurt like Tehran.

October 14

Last night, after I tossed and turned in bed for a while unable to sleep, I got lost in a YouTube wormhole trying to find Turkish political documentaries and ended up watching a Kurdish one called *A Fatal Dress Polygamy*, shot by a young Kurdish filmmaker named Mizgin Müjde Arslan whose family comes from that village. She went back to make this film about her aunt, Emine, who was sold to an old man before she was sixteen. The old man already had a couple of wives before her, and all together they made life a living hell for Emine. He beat Emine so much that she lost her mind. The pills that the psychiatrist prescribed paralyzed her. In the film, we only see Emine's feet shaking and flexing, as if wanting to get up and run but can't. The camera then asks the villagers about Emine. They tell us about how she used to be the most beautiful girl they had seen, how lively she once was.

It's a Kurdish village, so most of the film is in Kurdish with Turkish subtitles. Not all the cries of the Kurdish women are translated, but if anything, not knowing the meaning of all the words makes it more horrifying. Women's pain lies beneath the territories of countries, of languages we speak. Our pain is an underland of its own, with teeth and blood, raising us all together in its womb.

A cruel mother who then separates us, pits us against each other.

I cried for an hour, thinking about my earliest memory of my father hitting my mother. How she fell on her knees in the hallway, her lips bleeding, TV sounds in the background.

Then I put on the first episode of *Muhteşem Yüzyıl* in which Hürrem Sultan is brought to the palace as a slave. It worked like magic. After four episodes (eight and a half hours) I am finally sober, I think, less likely to break into tears any minute, and ready to sleep before I go to work in a few hours, even though my womb just started bleeding.

October 20

I've been working almost every day for the last two weeks. My exhaustion is highlighted today because at the end of my shift the head of the maids gave me a tour of every mistake I made cleaning the second floor, while a guest was in the kitchen listening to the whole thing and making sympathetic faces at me from where he sat. It was a golden moment for a story, but it sucked to be in it.

Treasures of the day:

3 euros' worth Pfand bottles

3 cents

October 25

Last night the doorbell rang for so long that I thought it was the fire alarm. I wasn't expecting anyone and of course Heidi and Victor weren't home. The mailman had not left any mail at our place for neighbors to pick up. I opened the door unwillingly and there was Eve crying, mascara and red rouge all over her face.

"Ah!" she screamed. "So happy you're home. Can I come in?"

But she was already taking off her high-heeled boots and beret as she asked. Without them she seemed so small, as if her body had shrunken into a little girl's. She threw herself on the kitchen couch.

"To think I sat through two Gaspar Noé films for him!" she said.

"To think I went there with a bottle of Dom Pérignon and wearing the most uncomfortable lingerie, sure he was going to give me an explanation for disappearing like that."

I pictured Eve with her cigarette and drink staring out the window half-naked, nodding, with a man from a Noé movie kicking walls in the background.

"Who would show up at someone's door this late?" Stefan asked her.

"I don't know," she said to him, "someone who lived with you for a month, who you told you loved, then stopped answering her texts for no reason?"

First, Stefan let Eve into his apartment, but he grabbed her wrist and kicked her out after she took his bike down from the wall and smashed it.

Sitting in a bar near his apartment, Eve texted him a long wrath asking how he could say she was a psycho when he could only have orgasms when Eve left her camera on. As he fucked her, he would ask Eve in his thick German accent if she was going to post their videos on Instagram. If she said no, he would beg her to do it. If she said yes, he would beg her not to. I have a wife, I have a religious mother, I have a reputation to protect, he would say, when in fact he had none of those things. He wanted Eve to tell him how pathetic he was, how he had the ugliest dick she had ever seen, how bad he smelled. The worst part was that he never acknowledged Eve's success when they had their clothes on. He told her Instagram was bound to be forgotten and so was she. She had to find a real job soon. Too bad she had all those gap years on her resume.

She took the Dom Pérignon out of her bag and asked if I had champagne glasses.

"I have two matching mugs," I said.

All night we talked about Stefan, much as I kept trying to change the subject and ask Eve questions about her Instagram projects and new apartment. Why had he worked so hard to make Eve fall for him, and when she finally did, get scared? Was Eve now supposed to forget she ever met this man and go on with her life or was she supposed to help Stefan overcome his insecurities and fear of commitment? Which one would make her a coward and which one would make her brave? What did being cowardly or brave have to do with love?

The more we drank, the more abstract our questions got. To me at least. The idea of Stefan became everything I once thought I wanted but sabotaged when I felt undesired or unfit like a master's degree or a writing career or a relationship. Not so sure about Eve. Eve doesn't make the connections I make between things that happen to her and memories, movies, herself. She sees every incident as its own. Like life is not a novel but a collection of short stories, and none of its heroines are responsible for the actions of the other ones, despite that fact that they're all written by the same person. I wonder if she feels lighter than I do inside. Stefan left her because he was scared of love. He said so before. So, his cowardice is to blame for Eve's sadness. But I can't point at anyone or anything for not letting me be happy. Not Berlin, not Turkey, not my university, not my friends, not my exes, not my father, not even myself.

It's only 8:00 a.m. Eve's asleep in my bed. I think I'll start walking to work now.

Being with other people makes me feel lonelier than being alone. Was it always like this or is this a new Leyla problem?

October 27

The bottom of my spine hurts. I try to use my sore body as a distraction from my irritated mind with little success. Two days ago, I fell off a chair while trying to open the window in the kitchen of our flat. I think the universe was punishing me because as I tried to pull the window open, I was contemplating telling Eve that she was too self-absorbed to ever find love.

Two days ago, I came home from work and found Eve passed out in my bed, holding a joint in one hand, her phone in the other. She'd kept all the doors open and windows closed so the whole flat smelled like weed and Vogues, when she knew none of my roommates smoked and we had a rule of never letting the flat smell like cigarettes.

Thinking about all this as if it were the end of the world, I fell and hit my head and the very end of my spine on the table and the floor. It hurt so much that I had to go to the ER. (Eve slept through it all.)

They put me in a waiting room with a woman who was playing Candy Crush with the sound on. My phone was dead, and I had nothing to read. My back hurt. My neck itched. I missed my mother.

A man in his fifties with a big belly and a white beard came out of the ER to the waiting room. The Candy Crusher asked him, "Did it hurt?"

"Yeah, like hell."

"Didn't they use anesthesia?"

"They did, that was the part that hurt the most."

They were both from the US and speaking in loud English. I justified not only listening but watching them like they were onstage by telling myself that they wanted it. I needed the diversion. The man kept walking around in the ER, as though he were avoiding sitting next to the woman. I tried to figure out what their relationship might be, the plot of their lives, the meaning of their stage directions.

The woman said, "I'm going to leave."

But she didn't. The man sat next to her. Then a new man came out of the ER and sat next to the two, across from me. He had the same finger as the first man bandaged. They looked at him. He looked at them. (I was invisible.)

"What did you do?" the new man asked, laughing. He was German.

The American said, "I was putting the dishes away and I tried to fit a bowl in a place it obviously didn't fit." He laughed, uncomfortably. "What about you?"

"I was climbing in the Caucasus Mountains a few days ago, and this one froze," the German answered, pointing at his smallest finger.

The Americans made sounds that implied they were shocked and impressed.

"I went to the hospital in Georgia and they treated it there right away. It was a common case there. I came back yesterday and wanted to go to a German doctor, too, just in case. But I think the doctors in Steglitz did something wrong. It's been getting worse since they touched it yesterday."

"Now I feel ashamed of my own injury. It's so not edgy compared to yours," the American said.

"No, don't say that. They probably hurt the same."

The woman asked, "So what did the doctors here say?"

"I won't die," said the German, smiling.

The woman said, "At least it's not a serious injury. Something a lot worse could have happened in that cold."

"They could have had to amputate it or something," the American man added.

The German said, "Well, actually, they said they might."

The Americans made sounds that implied they wanted to bury their heads under the ground. Their shared embarrassment started to melt the ice between the two.

A nurse called out my name, took an X-ray of my body, said nothing was broken, and sent me home with a few painkillers.

When I got back home, my room still smelled like Eve's cigarettes, but she was gone. I opened the windows, slowly this time. I told the Roomba to start cleaning. I emptied all the ashtrays Eve left behind. *Couldn't she have at least emptied them to help?* I thought. I changed the bedsheets. I swept off the loose pieces of tobacco and weed off the table, the couch, the bed, the floor. She took her empty Dom Pérignon bottle with her. *Of course,* I thought. *She's going to use it in five different Instagram posts, pretending it's a new bottle each time.* I checked the snack packs she brought with her for leftovers. She had eaten them all down to the last crumb. I binned them too and took the trash out.

Then, I found a note in my room, thanking me for being such a great friend and signed with love, which makes me feel like I am the one who's become too self-absorbed, cold-blooded, and distant to recognize intimacy.

November 11

11:11 was the name of a club in Istanbul before Gezi. Before first love and before its loss. Before a man with an AK-47 killed thirty-nine people dancing in Reina on a New Year's Eve. Before the Bosphorus Bridge turned into the 15 July Martyrs Bridge. Before we sold my childhood home to strangers and left without saying goodbye to anyone. Not even the Mediterranean, not even the stray dogs and cats, not even him who was already underground.

Anyway, it's past 12:12 now. And the club is long gone. We lost Beyoğlu long ago, in tear gas and water cannons.

I wonder what happened to Machine, that tiny club in a basement where Taksim met Tarlabaşı, where I took my first drugs. The DJ cabin was a cage, and people would try to climb in there at the end of the night. It felt safer than the outside world—until that night the police burst in with tear gas. It was our first time out clubbing after the long summer of Gezi protests. The streets had been calm for a couple weeks, and we'd all missed dancing so much. The ecstasy. We were punished immediately. We ran out of the basement like rats escaping exterminators. We coughed for days after and never went in there again.

November 20

On Saturday, after working the longest shift of the week without a break, I went out to a fancy restaurant followed by bars with Ash and his mother who was visiting from Dublin. We dropped the mother off at her hotel after she drank about fifteen mojitos to forget that her ex-husband is getting married to a younger woman and all her kids are spending Christmas with them instead of her.

Ash wanted to go clubbing. I hadn't been to a club since August. I had no desire to go, but what else was I going to do with my night? Ash said I didn't need to worry about money because he just got a promotion and he wanted to celebrate with a friend. I'd be doing him a favor. I feared that he'd never call me again if I turned him down. So, I said okay, but we got rejected at the door by three clubs, which never happened to me before. Maybe the clubs, too, can sense that Berlin doesn't want me anymore.

We settled for a bar across Wilden Renate, the last club that rejected us. Two sips into our beers, Ash left me alone with a gram of coke and went to have sex with a guy with whom he exchanged dick pics on Grindr. "I'll be back in twenty minutes. He lives around the corner," he said. I didn't hear from him for the next twenty-four hours.

I hooked up with a thirty-three-year-old Swedish right-wing conservative tourist. He's never taken drugs or smoked a cigarette in his life, and his favorite food is "American cuisine." Before he came over to my table and introduced himself, I was checking out the guy sitting next to him at the bar. But the Swede kept looking at me, not in a flirty way but as if I were someone he knew, like a friend of his grandmother. No, like he was a grandfather trying to remember whether I was a friend of his grandchild. Later he told me that the friend with whom he was traveling ditched him to go to a gay club with some guy he met at the bar and before he left, he told the Swede to come talk to me, the girl who was sitting alone in the corner. But the Swede couldn't see what I looked like without putting on his glasses, which his friend strictly told him not to.

When he came and said hi, I decided to talk to him because it seemed more fun than writing bad coked-up poetry on a bar napkin. But he wasn't giving me anything to work with. Talking to me about the Christmas market at Alexanderplatz? No coke? Not into techno? Not into art?

"What are you doing here?" I asked him.

The Swede laughed. His giant-like laughter echoed in the bar, which was now closing. I told him I wanted to go into Renate and wait for Ash there. This time we got in with no trouble. The Swede's straight face must have made me look less intoxicated too.

There we were, inside one of my favorite clubs, and I had coke left in my pocket. The old me would have run to the toilets, snorted a huge line, and danced for hours. The new me didn't even want to take her coat off. She felt like she was visiting the past. Except she was there with a two-meters-tall Swede with wide shoulders, the cleanest shave, and the most out-of-place way of talking and walking, like a good-hearted giant from a Grimms' fairy tale. It would have been ridiculous to see the Swede on the dance floor. I led us to the back room with the piano and whiskey bar. Two gin and tonics later, I asked him if we were going to have sex.

He said, "Yes, please."

Back in my room, I decided to take a line of coke, because why not? He didn't take any of course. I don't know for how long we had sex, but it was light outside when I said I couldn't do it anymore and he confessed he was exhausted too. Then, he said he hadn't had sex in two years. Two years!

Maybe because he got shy seeing my shocked face and wanted to change the subject, he asked if I was sleepy. I wasn't at all because I had been taking lines of coke all night or morning while we were having sex. I only had a little coke left and I thought if I left it for another night I'd want more and feel bad because I wouldn't be able to afford a resupply. Or this was my excuse to keep snorting during sex when the man I was having sex with had never seen coke in real life before. I had to do it. I couldn't know I had coke and not do it. Even though the sex was already great and the Swede was good-looking. I told him he could go to sleep, and I sat on my couch. I put my headphones on and listened to the oddest song one could listen to after a night like that. "Tanrı İstemezse" by Müslüm Gürses. Then I was ready to sleep too.

We woke up late in the afternoon and stayed in bed until late at night talking, having sex, talking. He told me about his life in Sweden working at the same Volvo branch since high school. His father, mother, and his father's father all used to work there as well. He would have been happy working there until his retirement, had it not been for the divorce. Now, he wanted something else but didn't know what.

"Divorce?" I asked surprised, without thinking.

I don't think I ever hooked up with a divorced man before. Not that I know of, at least. I was less startled by his divorce than I was dazed by my almost-seven-and-twenty years of age, like Anne Elliot in *Persuasion*. Is that next for me? The divorced? Men with kids?

The Swede's ex-wife was his high school sweetheart. Well, when they met, he was in high school and she was in middle school. By the time she was in high school, the Swede moved into his own place and the girl practically moved in with him. On his twenty-third birthday, he bought his own apartment with a Volvo-employee, special-rate mortgage deal and asked the girlfriend to marry him. The girlfriend, barely eighteen, happily agreed. They'd always talked about wanting to be young parents and they started trying as soon as the girl graduated from high school. After two years of not conceiving they went to see a doctor and found out the girl had a uterus illness that would make it hard to get pregnant. So began years spent on regular visits to the hospital, daily injections, false alarms. One day, the girl decided she needed a break from trying and went back to school. She was studying to be a kindergarten teacher. He was getting a new promotion every year. Maybe their child was waiting for the right time to join them. When the girl graduated from college, got all her certifications, and finally found a job as a teacher, she told him that she had to tell him something very important. Was she pregnant? Or maybe she was going to say she was ready to try again. Either way, he felt the news was going to be worth buying flowers for on the way home.

He knew something was wrong as soon as he turned his key in the lock. The girl had packed a big suitcase and was sitting on the couch, silently waiting. Neither the TV nor any music was on. She started crying when she saw him. He started apologizing, not knowing what he did but sure he had done something wrong without realizing it.

"Because she was perfect," he said. "The perfect wife."

As it turned out, the perfect wife had been cheating with a friend from college. It was nothing serious, it was already over, but she felt ashamed and could not look into the Swede's eyes. Now, he was crying too.

"There's something else that I need to tell you," his wife then told the Swede. "I'm pregnant. Either one of you could be the father."

And so began the strangest year of his life. He convinced the wife to stay with him and not to take a DNA test until the baby was born, though the other potential father knew about the pregnancy as well. Both men and both of their families half prepared for this baby as if it were their own. When the Swede woke up and felt his wife's growing belly next to his own body, he was the happiest man on earth. When he was driving to work, he started crying, picturing his wife and the baby with another man in another car. Something started to crack inside the Swede.

(He didn't say it like that, though.) (That was me, imagining how he must have felt, projecting my own cracked insides every time I imagine my two potential futures in Turkey or Germany.)

When the baby was born, both men were waiting outside the door. The nurse told both that they had a son.

"For two days I had a son," he said. "Two days later, I had no son and no wife."

There he was, thirty-one, single, not a young father. He realized he'd lost his chance to have his only dream in life come true. He'd never made any backup plans for happiness. He had no idea about what to do with himself. It took him two years to smile again.

"I'm so sorry," I said. And then, "I'm so sorry you had to go through all of that. I truly am, but did anybody tell you how much this all sounds like a soap opera?"

"No, no one did. Do you watch a lot of soaps?"

"Too much," I said. "It's my guilty pleasure."

"Guilty pleasure?" he asked. "What does that mean?"

"It's what English speakers say about things they're ashamed of enjoying. Like soap operas or country music or reality TV."

"Ha," he said. "Why would anyone be ashamed of enjoying something?" And then, "How come you're so American?"

"Don't call me that," I said.

Then, I told him about all the American schools my family sent me to in Turkey so that I could be more successful in life. How it only took the child Leyla a few months to get high on American culture, the English language. It had made me feel special to live a parallel life within Turkey, speaking another language so well, reading books without translations, watching movies without subtitles, listening to all the cool songs and being able to sing along. When I finally found my way back into my own culture in shisha bars and went against my parents' will to the arabesque music halls I frequented in college, I felt disobedient. For a long time, the dissonance felt like a drug replacing America in my mind. Although, of course, not entirely, because I went to an American university and most of my friends liked chai tea lattes more than Turkish tea, Beirut the band more than any band from Lebanon. We'd all traveled to more cities abroad than in Turkey, more countries in the West than the Middle East.

"How did you end up working as a cleaner?" the Swede asked. "Sounds like you come from money."

And so, I found myself telling this stranger about my father's death, the debts he left behind, the collapse of the Turkish economy, the Gezi protests, my lucky escape. I told him how losing everything made me realize I'd never earned the privileges I once had in the first place.

He laughed another giant's laugh and asked, "So you're here to repent for things you had no control over? Did you sentence yourself to cleaning the way they make petty criminals clean the streets in American series?"

"No! Yes. Maybe?" I said. "It's not like I chose to be a cleaner. But if I ever find my way out of this mess, I'll know better than to close my eyes again."

Then I told him I'd get dressed and make pasta. I was starving. We hadn't eaten anything all day.

He said, "Let's order burgers."

"Didn't you hear the story I just told you?"

"I did, but I really need to eat a burger now."

It had been months since I last ate a burger. I wanted to say yes. But would I have to pay for it? He did pay for the gin and tonic and insisted on taking a taxi home and paying for it last night. But we were still in Germany after all. If I had to pay for a burger it would mean I couldn't buy wine until the end of the month.

"Don't worry I'll pay," he said. "I saved up all my life for a baby that's now somebody else's. I can buy you a burger."

I didn't resist. When the burger came, we sat up on the bed and ate like a couple of wild animals. The meat, the cheese, the sauce, it all felt so good in my mouth.

Then he looked at me very carefully and said, "You know, you would never have asked me if we were going to have sex if we talked a little longer at the bar."

"Why?"

"You're a real leftist. I'm a conservative. I'm not far right, but I'm on the right side."

What was I supposed to do with that information?

"Are you against taking refugees and immigrants into Europe?" I asked.

"I'm here with you, aren't I?" he asked.

He explained that his right-wing concerns were only on the economic side of things. He said Sweden asked for too much tax and some other things I didn't want to listen to.

I said, "Hey, we're only having a one-night stand. It's not like we're getting married. I don't need to know everything about you."

"Can I tell you one last thing?"

"Do you want to have more sex or not?"

"You're the only person I've ever had sex with other than my ex-wife."

"Oh," I said. "I don't even know how many people I've had sex with."

"Oh, I for sure don't want to know that," he said.

He will come back and stay with me over Christmas. Part of me wants to marry him and call it a life.

Yesterday Eve picked me up from work, dragged me home, forced me to take a shower, put on my dress, and go to Karstadt where I had drunkenly confessed to her once that I sometimes go to put on Chanel N°5 and smell like a past version of myself: the seventeen-year-old Leyla who could buy whatever she wanted with her father's money. The Leyla who was so impatient to grow up she wore high heels and got manicures every weekend. A Leyla none of my Berlin friends would recognize.

"Trust me, for this surprise you will want to smell like Chanel," Eve said.

Then, she took me to an art opening in the west, way west. It was a hotel-themed group exhibition. A French photographer had a collection of photographs taken at hotels in different parts of the world. An American painter painted about thirty imagined hotel rooms—kids jumping on the bed throwing confetti around in one (I immediately imagined the unimagined cleaner of that room and it gave me enormous anxiety to think about how frustrating it would be to clean small pieces of the confetti stuck and hidden in every corner of the room) or sexy women reading books in bathrobes on the balcony looking out at the moon. And then there was a German artist, who re-created miniatures of the most famous hotels in history that no longer exist. Too many people were in there holding Sekt glasses for me to survive without drinking myself. But a glass of Sekt was 6 euros—6!

"What's the surprise?" I asked Eve.

"This is it," she said. "I thought you would appreciate being here."

"Oh," I said. I didn't want to break her spirits. "I do. Thank you!"

She giggled and said, "Of course I'm joking. There's a man here I want you to meet. The German painter. I met him at a bar last night and when he told me about his work, I told him about yours. Your cleaning job and your writing."

"My writing?"

"Your diary. I told him it's a book and that he could learn from you."

I'd read Eve the first couple of pages from my diary, but it was months ago and we were both drunk.

"He invited both of us here tonight and said he'd be interested in working with you. Isn't that exciting?"

I'm not going to lie. I got excited. Even though his art was not impressive, to say the least. We waited for over an hour for him to come to us, but he didn't acknowledge Eve beyond a cold smile, which made her pretty angry, and I realized we were not there for me.

"Let's get out of here," Eve said abruptly when I was in the middle of a conversation with a middle-aged woman about whether good art should have a purpose. Art for art's sake is a privilege only Westerners with money have I was telling the woman. Eve likes that I'm her political friend, but she mostly turns to her phone when I talk about the distribution of power and wealth, unless she can find an opening in the conversation where she can rail against the power dynamics between her and her romantic interests, which is good enough, because that's also political.

"I'm sorry I dragged you all the way here," she said. "I thought he meant what he said. But I will make it up to you. I have an idea."

On the U-Bahn back to my apartment she said I should do a bar reading and read from my diary. She said I could make some money out of it. At first, I dismissed it. But this morning I found myself reading and rereading what I've been writing in this notebook. Eve was right. I don't know if this is a book, but it looks like I've been writing to be read by others.

But where can I do it? Not at Giovanni's. Thinking about that room reminds me of my history of quitting all that I was once passionate about, leaving everything unfinished. I haven't talked to Giovanni since September. I'd meant to tell him I gave up on finding Christiane F. and didn't want to interview anyone else but never had the courage, and too much time has passed now. The only bars I went to in the last year were places that are already hosting their own bad monthly reading series. And all those places hate me because Aria and I always sneak in a wine bottle and drink from it, even though we've been warned by the bartenders more than once. This will have to wait. My next Ausländerbehörde appointment is less than a month away so I need to stay focused on the case. The court could respond to my appeal any day now.

I have to leave for work soon and leave Eve in my bed again. I wonder if she's been reading my diary when she's alone in my room. I know she went through all the drawers, boxes, and notebooks in most of her exes' apartments. I wouldn't be too surprised if she has been doing the same here. I think I would kind of like it.

November 27

Last night, on Eve's advice, I skipped the first seventy pages of *My Brilliant Friend* and started reading again from the part where they become teenagers. It's strange that reading about the teenage years was easier than reading about childhood, since my teen years were worse than my childhood. But that's what I did all night—and morning and afternoon—until now. I took a break from reading thirty pages before the book's end. Elena's poor Neapolitan neighborhood, built and enclosed with violence and misfortune instead of bricks, feels like home. I want to stay there for a little longer.

It's comforting to read novels narrated from the future selves of their characters. Even in the most desperate acts of a story, we know that the narrator will survive in the end and make it far enough to write a novel.

Will I ever be able to write about these days from a safe distance? Can Ferrante show me the way out of this paralysis, self-censorship, self-sabotage? Can I then imagine speaking with my mother and sister for more than a couple of minutes without finding a reason to raise my voice and eyebrows?

Maybe. But today, I can't afford to buy the sequel to *My Brilliant Friend*. *The Story of a New Name* costs more than six bottles of Aldi wine and six weeks' worth of Aldi potatoes combined.

November 30

Some days I can go as far as to say that I like my job. I can think of whatever I want while doing it. And sometimes I hate it for this, but I'm thankful that human interaction is at a minimum. Most of the time it's me, my vacuum cleaner, and my music.

When I can't help what I'm thinking, I listen to old Turkish songs and imagine myself in an old Turkish movie. Today, I couldn't stop listening to Cem Karaca's "Tamirci Çırağı." A mechanic's apprentice narrates a whole story in the song. He falls in love with a rich girl who drops off her car at their shop and says he'd read it in a novel once that a girl like her somehow fell for an apprentice like him. On the day she's coming to pick up her car, the apprentice asks his master, *Can I please not wear the overalls today?* He combs his hair and waits breathlessly. The girl walks in the door and time stops for the apprentice. But when he opens the car's door for her, she asks, eyebrows raised, *Who's this bum?* She drives off, drowning the apprentice in her exhaust. The master pets the back of the drowning boy. *Forget novels,* he says. *You're a worker, stay a worker, put on those overalls.*

If I'd met the Swede when I was seventeen, he'd be the mechanic's apprentice in this story. He was training to become a Volvo salesman back then, and I was my father's little rich girl. No one had told me these roles could be reversed in an instant. But I was undoubtedly the apprentice in the music video I directed in my mind today while I cleaned after cheap hostel boarders. The Swede was the rich girl, but instead of raising his eyebrows, he opened his car's door for me to get in. I didn't.

A memory I haven't thought of in years just flashed into my mind: one afternoon during elementary school, our homeroom teacher told us that in Europe, you could see a lawyer marrying a garbage collector, because everyone, including garbage collectors, were educated there. There were no class inequalities when it came to survival and education. A garbage collector was a garbage collector because he chose to be. Was she right, or has her misguided fiction been writing my life in Berlin all this time? It is true that I've never felt a class divide here like I did in Turkey. But is that in fact because I am among the lowest now and, like the mechanic, I can't even see the rich I cross paths with for what they are anymore? What does it matter? I make the same amount of money as my high school best friend who's a lawyer in Turkey, and I get to live here, walk in parks with friends, wine bottles in our hands, wearing our invisibility cloaks. It's easier to be who we are when no one's looking. Yes, invisibility is a superpower that the bourgeoisie and the so-called grounded ones forgot to take from us: the cleaners, mechanic's apprentices, delivery heroes. Let them starve their souls working in the slaughterhouses disguised as modern offices. Let them be miserable in the cities they're born to and torment themselves over what others would think of them if they ever tried to make it elsewhere and failed. We may not have money, we may not have visas, but we have the streets to walk as who we are.

December 1

After I waxed poetic about how much I like my job for a whole page yesterday, I went to work this morning to a stinging surprise. Apparently, the head of the maids thinks I'm such a bad cleaner that she assigned Ali to train me one more time.

This time, Ali showed me his best tricks to make the head of the maids leave him alone.

1. Complain about the guests being extra dirty half an hour into the shift, even if they aren't, which they probably are. This will make her expect less from you.

2. If she's in the room, fold the blankets exactly the way she does. Stand on the right side on the bed and say ein, zwei, drei with each fold. Easing her OCD is your best shot at making her like you.

3. If she's not around, only vacuum windowsills and wall corners. She barely ever looks at the actual floor. This will help you not break your back trying to vacuum under the beds and lockers of twenty rooms every single day.

4. Skip the pink spray when cleaning the bathrooms. It's bad for your skin and who knows what it does to your insides. Just use the blue spray. It makes everything shine no matter what anyway. This will save you at least ten minutes every time.

5. Listen to Turkish music. She hates Turkish music. It works like Raid.

December 8

Two days ago, the court sent both me and the university copies of the same letter, advising us to meet and discuss the case one last time before they set a hearing. Yesterday, the university sent me an invitation email to meet the director in his office at the end of January. The court wants us to solve the issue among ourselves since I'm on legal aid and if a hearing takes place and I lose, the government will have to cover the expenses. The letter clearly states that if the director wants to give me another chance to write this thesis, there isn't a law that prohibits them from doing so. I'm a student who's now proven that she really wants another chance to study; they're professors who must have had some interest in teaching me at one point at least, right? All they have to say is OK. Okay. Ok.

December 10

There's a bedbug infestation on the top floor of the hostel, so we had to climb up and down five floors, carrying trash bags full of bedsheets, mattress covers, and pillows all day.

We're supposed to call them by their code name, hats, so that guests don't freak out and cancel their bookings when they hear the word "bedbug."

"In fact," the head of the maids explained cheerfully, "this is a great opportunity for Putzis to participate in the hostel's fun activities. If anyone hears you mention hats, you can let them know that we've hid pictures of little hats in the lobby, and whoever finds one gets a free drink from the Mad Hatter, the bartender."

"Fuck that," Ali said when she left the room. Mia and I nodded in bitter agreement. Not only do we have to risk carrying the little assholes into our apartments with no extra pay, but the sneaky management wants to give us more tasks so they can offer more free entertainment to their cheap-ass guests too?

I washed my clothes twice when I came back home. In the shower, I thought about the days when I was a pot-smoking, mushroom-taking, pretend hippie like the guests that come to stay at our hostel. I remembered this one coffee shop in Amsterdam. What was the name? Impossible to recall. There's too much fog around memories from my early twenties. But it was a small, cozy coffee shop with tables shaped like mushrooms from Alice in Wonderland. Yet, they sold a strain of weed called AK-47, the violence of which never bothered me until now.

How easy it is to trick people! You just have to throw in a couple of sweet pop culture references in the same bag with a couple of controversial ones, and voilà, you have a product, ready to be devoured by tourists who think they've found their very own personal Wonderland!

Little do they know, not only their Wonderland but the whole world is infested with bedbugs. The Mad Hatter is underpaid, the Cat is overworked, and Alice's visa is running out.

December 13

It's before 9:00 a.m. and before coffee. As an act of rebellion against the fear of losing things, I cut my own hair. It's too short and uneven. I'm going to the Ausländerbehörde today to apply for an extension on my Fiktionsbescheinigung.

December 14

I just had a dream in which I woke up in a room that was not my own but was mine. It looked like my old room in Istanbul but not quite the same. I stepped outside. The hallway led to our kitchen here, but the door was on the wrong side. Our photos were still up on the fridge, but the fridge was so dirty it turned gray and took the colors of our pictures with it. The chairs I'd found on the street were there, but on them sat three strangers. I think that German guy Victor had over a few months ago was one of them. The other two were strangers, but they all looked alike. The apartment was dirty; no one had cleaned it for years. The unwashed dishes rose like a mountain, garbage bags on the kitchen table were three other mountains, the bottles on the floor were like a river that drew the border between me and my room, the one I'm writing this from. I could almost smell my past decomposing. The strangers weren't even looking at me. I wanted to ask them what they were doing in my apartment, but there was no air in my lungs. No sound came out.

I woke up from my dream so thirsty I ran to the kitchen with my eyes barely open. I drank three big glasses of water and came back into my room.

Heidi came with me to the Ausländerbehörde as my poor volunteer interpreter. I was so nervous that I couldn't say a word on the way to Keplerstrasse. We entered the room where two immigration officers sat at their desks. The woman on the right told us to sit with her and asked for my documents. I handed her my neatly organized documents immediately. She asked me a couple of questions that I was almost certain I understood and answered correctly with a ja or nein. She turned to her computer and we sat in silence for the longest few minutes of my life. Was she the same woman from June? It was hard to tell. But she had the same cold, serious expression on her face, as if she were not looking at the files of a human being but instead trying to find and exterminate a bedbug on her bed, a rat in her building, a virus in her system.

She asked me how I managed to get by with only 600 euros a month. I started answering in English, but she stopped me.

"Kannst du nicht deutsch sprechen?"

"Ich kann, aber nicht sehr gut, wenn ich nervous bin."

Then, I think, she told me I had to speak German if I wanted to stay in Germany. Maybe she asked why I wanted to stay in Germany if I didn't even speak any German. Or maybe the question was how I thought I could stay in Germany if I didn't want to learn German. I tried to speak.

"Ich . . . Ich . . . Ich . . ."

I couldn't.

My cheeks got so red and hands so sweaty and heartbeat so fast it was louder than all my attempts to speak in German. I don't know what I would say if I could say it. I couldn't think. I could only feel the guilt for not being able to speak the language of the city I call home. I remembered the word for "guilt" in German and how it also means debt I think. Schuld. They were all looking at me: Heidi, the woman, and the man who sat at the desk across from us. Eventually, the woman turned to Heidi and they talked among themselves until Heidi told me it was time for us to go outside and wait for the decision in the hall.

Now my heart's beat was replaced by the sound of the clock. I don't know how long we waited. Maybe ten minutes, maybe an hour. No one dared to say a word.

Back in the room, the same woman said to me in fluent English: "Here, we've granted you a six-month extension, but unless you win your case against the university or find a job that fulfills the work visa requirements for Turkish citizens, don't come back for another extension. This is your last chance."

I took my Fiktionsbescheinigung like a bride taking the marriage certificate from the officer who marries them in a soap.

It's not like I didn't want to learn German. I took two German courses when I first moved. I tried speaking to shopkeepers in German. I watched German movies. I even listened to German rap. I thought that if I learned German, I could maybe unlearn Turkish and this American English. I wanted to forget all the lies I've been told in these languages, all the losses I've cried for. I knew Berlin was the perfect place to do this since the first day I came here as a tourist. You didn't see a Starbucks at every corner here. You didn't see flags of any country, especially Germany's.

Germans faced and paid for their crimes against humanity. People could say whatever they wanted here now (except the two *h* words next to one another of course) and dress however they pleased, dance for as long as their feet would carry them. I couldn't wait to move here and learn German.

On my first morning as a Berlin resident, I'd walked into a Bäckerei in Neukölln to get a coffee and a croissant. The owner was of course Turkish, and he'd asked me if I was a tourist from Istanbul. When I told him I'd just moved here, he asked about my family. He was startled when I told him they lived in Turkey. He asked what I was going to do in gurbet all alone hem de kız başıma. He said Turkey was doing great thanks to the AKP and there was no reason to suffer in this cold country. I asked him why he was here then. He frowned his eyebrows and raised his voice. He said it was too late for him to go back now; his business was here, his kids were here, his home was here. I told him it wasn't as great as he thinks to live in Turkey, took my coffee and croissant, and left. Walking back home I couldn't get the sounds of Turkish politicians yelling at each other on the news out of my head. I couldn't stop thinking about prisons filled with writers, activists, students. I thought about my old boss in Turkey who screamed at one of us every day. I thought about my father who roared in anger at his employees, his family, and himself all his life. I decided it would be best if I stayed away from Turks for a while.

But every German shopkeeper I tried to speak in German to responded as if it was impossible to hear what I was saying through my accent. Friends I tried to speak with in German started correcting me at "hallo." Every German I met in a bar wanted to talk to me about Erdoğan, Islam, Kurdistan. (I wanted to talk about these, too, but there was something that made me feel uncomfortable when talking about them with Westerners.) (I hadn't realized yet that was their own guilt projected on me.) One German I hooked up with asked me what my family back in Turkey would do if they knew about my lifestyle in Berlin. Once, in a club, a German guy asked my circle of friends where everybody came from. I was with Aussie, Irish, and Swedish friends. To everyone he said, "Oh wow" and "Cool." When I told him I was from die Türkei he said, "Oh no." Finally, one night, walking to the U-Bahn after work with my manager at my first job here, I was casually asked not to speak Turkish in the office building. Not even when I spoke to my family on my lunch break. It made people uncomfortable not knowing what I was talking about. "Especially the older colleagues, you know," she said. "Try to understand them. They're from another era."

My mother tongue made Germans uncomfortable, yet as a Turk trying to speak German, I was only a Turk trying to speak German. When I spoke in English, I was an expat speaking better English than most Europeans, including my professors. Some of them couldn't hear my accent and thought I was American. Some of them assumed I was Portuguese because of my good English despite my dark skin. When I told them I was Turkish, they said, "No, you don't look Turkish at all," as if it were a compliment.

They asked fewer questions about Turkey, more about my writing, the art I liked, what I wanted from life. Sure, some people still asked me questions about headscarves, but more often than not I was seen as a bohemian creative who came to Berlin to work on her art rather than a poor Turk to whom Germany granted a chance for a new life but who clearly didn't belong here, since she couldn't so much as speak German.

I wasn't thinking about any of this yesterday, though. Heidi and I were both so happy on the way back home. We stopped at Lidl to buy fruits (for her) and chocolate (for me). I also got candles and white roses. Heidi made tea and I made coffee. We sat on our kitchen couch, listening to Mercan Dede and Kraftwerk. Even Victor, who was working from home, came out of his room and ordered food for us all. In the afternoon, I invited Eve, Defne, Aria, and Ash for drinks. I baked a chocolate cake. Heidi and Victor joined too. We smoked, drank, and talked for hours. I wished that the woman at the Ausländerbehörde could see us. This was the answer to her question: this apartment, the table I found on the street on a Sunday and carried here with Victor, washed in the shower, painted with Heidi, around which we speak our own mix of English, Turkish, Spanish, and German and understand each other better than most would do in our own languages.

December 15

Today after work, instead of taking the train back home I went to Tempelhof, my first neighborhood in Berlin. I hadn't been to Scardanelli since I moved, but I was hoping Yvonne still worked there so I could talk to her about doing a reading.

When I arrived, she was opening the bar. We hugged and caught up while she turned on the lights, opened the register, put new candles on the bottles on each table and lit them, then poured us two Mexikaners. Yvonne is one of those people who overwhelm you with wholeness, a dancer and soon-to-be dietician from South Africa. Well, she was born here but spent most of her life in Johannesburg where her family's from. Back when I was at Sisyphos every weekend, we'd run into each other on the dance floor almost every Sunday. We'd often both be on our own. She came to the club to dance only. She didn't drink or take anything. I'd be as high as one could be. I'd usually stay after my friends left the club and wait for new friends to arrive the next day. So Yvonne and I would not talk a lot, but we'd dance together for sometimes hours at a time. She always gave me free shots when I stopped by at Scardanelli to say hi, until that night she had to carry me to my apartment when I was too drunk and high on ketamine to walk up the stairs. I don't remember much from that night, but I remember falling off the stool while talking to a hot tourist who then quickly decided to call it a night. I also remember Yvonne tucking me in and looking at me like she was mourning my soul, which now belonged to Berlin, like I was a lost cause, a tranquilized body, mind removed.

I didn't go back to the bar after that. At first because I thought she'd judged me that night. She was jealous of my ability to let go, when she always had to eat healthy, stay sober, study hard, be in control of her life. Then, I didn't go back because seeing myself through her eyes made my fall too clear. We stopped dancing together in the club. I avoided her favorite room and she mine. When we ran into each other in the garden, we each said a faint hello with a fainter smile. But today was different. I was ready and excited to go there, show her I still have a soul, I survived the dark rooms, I am still creating, and I am still here.

She was warm and welcoming to me, but I knew something was up with her when she poured us two new shots. I had to ask what was wrong.

"This is my last week working here," she said.

"Why?"

She had been working at Scardanelli since before I moved to Berlin.

"Long story."

"You know I love long stories."

"You're lucky," she said. "You have Kreuzberg, Wedding, even Neukölln. I have nowhere in Berlin. Nowhere is safe for us."

About three weeks ago, their neighbors found her boyfriend unconscious in front of the building they had just
moved into. He was beaten so badly that he had to stay in
the hospital for over a week. He had internal bleeding and
bruises all over his body. Thankfully, his head was alright,
except for a swollen eye and split lips. He told Yvonne
and the police that three skinheads attacked him out of
nowhere when he was trying to unlock his own front door.
They called him all the worst possible names and told him
to go back to where he came from or the next people who
saw him might not be as merciful as they were.

"We know your address," they said. "But you won't
live here for much longer, will you?"

This all happened on Karl Marx Allee, the middle of
Friedrichshain. I didn't know what to say. Yvonne rolled
herself a cigarette and asked if I wanted one too. I said
yes. We smoked in silence.

Then she told me why she was quitting Scardanelli.
When she told Günter, her boss, what happened, he asked
Yvonne: "Are you sure they were skinheads? It sounds a bit
suspicious to me. These things don't happen in Germany
anymore. And certainly not in the center of Berlin. Maybe
he was mixed up in some other business that he's not telling you about. You're a good girl from South Africa with
a good education and parents, you don't know enough
about the Africans here. I felt something was off about
that guy the first time I met him."

"I don't know how what happened next happened,"
Yvonne told me. "I started yelling every single racist thing

he told me since I started working here. All his words I'd tried so hard to ignore and forget came out of me like a tsunami. I talked and talked and talked. He looked at me in denial but also pity, as though I didn't know what I was saying. No, it was disgust. The more he looked, the more I said. When I said everything, I added, 'I quit.'"

Yvonne then stormed out of the bar and went back to the hospital to her boyfriend. But the next day, the boss called her and apologized.

"I'm sorry if I offended you," Günter said. "It was never my intention to do so. I understand if you want to quit working for me. But please at least stay until I find someone new. I know you need the money too."

She had told him she needed extra shifts for extra money to support her boyfriend right before he stated his racist concerns. She said yes since the boss rarely came to the bar anyway. But he just found a replacement for her, so she won't be coming to work after Monday.

If I were capable of crying in front of others I would have.

"What are we even doing here?" I asked her.

"Hey," she said. "Don't speak like that. It's what they want. We're here because we want to be. I'm a German citizen for God's sake! My boyfriend never left Europe in his life, and you deserve to be here as much as we do, any French writer or Dutch DJ."

"I'm sorry, it's me who should be cheering you up," I said. "Do you remember that time we danced for ten hours and then walked to the train together? The sunrise?"

As we recalled the waking sky we walked under, I felt the unexpected July breeze back on my neck again. There was nothing extraordinary about that particular sunrise. Nothing wild had happened that night to either of us. We didn't say much while we walked. But we both couldn't stop smiling. We asked each other why we were smiling and both said, "Keine ahnung!" We started laughing, then dancing to our laughter and the silence of the streets and pointing at different colors in the sky until we split ways.

When the Berlin sky shows you its beauty, you can't let being sleepless, tired, or sad stop you from taking it in. You have to look up so you can remember it at times like this, in the cold winter nights sworn to keep all colors out of sight, even when we need them the most.

Then, customers started coming in, Yvonne had to work, the music got louder, and I left.

Now, I definitely want to find a place to read from my diary. But it has to be a woman-and-immigrant-owned bar. And it has to be within the borders of Kreuzkölln.

December 18

Treasures of the day:

A leather bracelet to give the Swede as a
    Christmas present

3 cents

Five Berliner Kindls

8 euros' worth of Pfand bottles.

I had thirty-three checkouts. I didn't clean all the rooms
as thoroughly as I should have, and now it's 9:00 p.m. and
I'm thinking about this.

Is anxiety a punishment capitalist gods invented for
lazy cleaners?

December 26

I didn't take my free beers home today since my fridge is already full of beer the Swede bought for us on Christmas. He left this morning, and I went to work. I was right on time but an hour late. I thought I was working at 11:00 a.m. like every other day, but apparently I'd signed up for a new shift that starts at 10:00. They called me twenty-eight times before I picked up the phone but didn't seem mad when I got there.

I need to overcome my soap opera addiction ASAP. It was easy to abstain when the Swede was around. I only thought about it once or twice. But as I write these lines, I'm streaming my third show in the background.

On Christmas, Victor and I invited Defne over for dinner. Heidi and pretty much everyone else we know in Berlin went home to their families. Defne, Victor, and I all started celebrating Christmas only after we moved to Berlin. For us, it's just another day to meet and eat together. And an excuse for Victor to buy more plastics from Ikea. I hadn't thought about what it would mean to someone like the Swede until he told me this was the first Christmas ever that he wouldn't be spending with his mother. Under normal circumstances, she would have never let him spend it in another country, away from her, but this year was different.

This year, she was happy he was with me because it was the first time he's been happy since his divorce.

In Berlin, we're all professionals at hiding the fact from one another that we have feelings, until we take some kind of drug, which makes us spill our deepest, darkest secrets on the table and announce that our companions are our new best friends, which is usually followed by avoiding contact with the audience of our emotional declarations for as long as we can. This strange Swede, though, is never afraid of saying what he feels. Spending time with him makes me more honest, too, and it feels new and familiar at the same time, like a happy memory that comes to mind after hours of turning in bed alone worrying about the future wide awake.

I told him he could come back and celebrate New Year's Eve with us too. He booked his ticket before he left.

I walked him to the U-Bahn station at Kottbusser Tor when he was leaving for the airport. Before he got on the train, he turned around and said, "I love you." Who does that? In Berlin, no one. He had already said "I love you" during sex on the first night we met. And that was weird enough for a Berlin girl, but this?

I walked back home trying to focus on the rooms I'll have to clean tomorrow.

December 27

Today at lunch, Ali said that the system here only benefits bad people. That's why only bad people from Turkey can make it here.

Last month, his coffee shop boss asked Ali to work extra shifts at the Christmas market booth. Ali couldn't do it since he would be exceeding the twenty hours he's legally allowed to work and the boss didn't want to pay him under the table. So, Ali recommended his friend Mert, a German Turk who had never worked before, since his parents paid his rent and he always received generous government grants to study. Mert was only twenty, and they knew each other from the clubbing scene, but Ali always thought Mert was very mature for his age. He wanted to help Mert see what real life was like. The kid had the newest iPhone and wore sneakers every weekend, but he never seemed to have money when it came to paying for the gram. Ali convinced him to take the job and save money for the holiday season. Mert agreed reluctantly.

The boss liked Mert so much that he asked him to work shifts at the coffee shop too. Ali was surprised when Mert accepted, since Mert always said he didn't want or need to work. Ali was excited to work with a friend, but soon he realized that Mert was an entirely different person at work. He started ordering Ali around and pointing out his every mistake. When Ali told him to back off, Mert said he was only trying to help so things worked better. Ali was slow and messy. He knew this himself. If the boss wasn't around, he didn't clean the bathrooms every hour, and he didn't do rounds to collect empty cups from tables. Instead, he spent most of his time on Snapchat and flirting with cute customers. But people liked him. The regulars knew his name, he knew theirs. He learned who liked which kind of complimentary cookies with their coffee, which color of sugar. He remembered people's favorite songs and played them. Even the most serious old Germans laughed at his jokes. He loved starting his days in the coffee shop, behind the counter. It felt like his stage—before Mert ruined it all.

Yesterday when his boss came to the shop, Ali asked him not to give Mert and him the same shifts. His boss asked why. Ali said it wasn't what he imagined working with a friend would be like. Why, the boss asked again, but he didn't wait for Ali's answer. Instead, raising his voice with every word, he told him he knew why. He had been watching Ali through the camera, he knew how Ali was slacking, and Mert didn't want to let him. Yes, Mert told him everything. He also told him that Ali worked a third job as a delivery guy under the table. It was bad enough Ali's work at the hostel kept getting in the way of taking on extra shifts but watching through the camera how Ali rushed out without finishing his end-of-shift tasks for a job he wasn't legally allowed to do—the boss couldn't tolerate this much, certainly not for someone who didn't do half of what he was getting paid for. He was fired.

Ali wanted to punch Mert's big nose then and there, but Mert was twice his size. Instead, he took his jacket and stormed out. In the afternoon, Mert came to Ali on campus, as if nothing had happened. When Ali asked how he could do that to him, Mert said he had no choice. This wasn't Turkey. Germans were raised with work ethics, and he had to do the right thing. He told Ali not to take it personally. He had no trace of guilt on his face when he said it.

I wondered how much it really had to do with the system that Ali lost his job or that I am losing my visa and how much of it was our fault. I didn't tell him this of course. I'm not German. But I thought about it for the rest of my shift. Did this question come to my mind because I've been living as a failed thesis for so long that I've internalized I deserve this punishment? Or is it the truth? Does Ali deserve to be fired for not doing exactly as he was ordered? Is it so wrong to want to make a little room for your shape in a system rather than shaping yourself to fit into it? What qualifies as making it in this system?

January 3

The Sky

I'm on a flight to Gothenburg, but first things first. Today was a good day. The head of the maids was on holiday. I only worked for five hours and found a lot of treasures left behind by guests who checked out after New Year's Eve.

Treasures of the new year:

12 euros' worth Pfand bottles

One big bottle of Jägermeister—only barely consumed

Half a bottle of Gordon's

Two bottles of Apfelschorle

An expired but unopened cheese plate from Albert Heijn

(I don't like any of these things, but Heidi loves them all and doesn't believe in expiration dates.)

I suspect the head of the maids checks the rooms before all of us in the mornings when she's here and takes all the best stuff for herself. But I have no proof. Also, I'm only half-serious and maybe this theory says more about me than it does about her.

I barely spent any money this week. Last night, Defne came over with surprise ketamine. I had wine left over from the Swede and found a quarter-full tube of coke in my room after New Year's Eve. We had it all. Except we both knew in the morning I would have to go clean toilets and she would go clean the cybertrash that washes up on the shores of Berlin's skyscrapers.

She came with a big bag to stay indefinitely. She'd hooked up with her roommate the night before his girlfriend came to visit for a month, so she didn't want to be home. I was planning to rent out my room while I was gone to make a little money, but I couldn't turn Defne away. It feels as though I'm watching myself break when I see her.

When I used to work where she works, all I ever wanted was to have fun. Fun meant not thinking about the torture videos, pedophiles, self-harm. I never had thoughts about harming myself. One could argue I wasn't thinking of self-harm because I was already doing it, by using the razor to cut lines instead of myself. But Defne straight out started having dreams in which she was doing to herself what the girls she saw do in videos at work. She wouldn't tell me what they were. But she did tell me she started having similar visions when she was awake. She stopped going to classes. She ditched her new boyfriend she was so excited about before I could meet him so I can't be sure who was to blame for the big fights that led to their breakup, but I have a feeling it's the job's fault. When your job is driving you mad and you can't face it because then you'd have to quit and search for another job that will most probably also drive you mad or poison you, you need to take your anger out on someone. Anyone. Whoever is the closest to you.

The Applicant

* * *

This is the first of two trips I will make to Sweden within two weeks. I will come back to Berlin for four days in between because the beds, floors, and toilets of the hostel won't clean themselves.

What if they don't let me back into Germany on Saturday because of this fictional visa I have? The woman at the Ausländerbehörde did say I could travel with it. I'm so tired of the anxiety that is attached to my passport.

I have 100 euros in my account now for the rest of the month, but the seat I am sitting on costs 300. What a life.

I spent New Year's Eve in my bedroom with the Swede, all my best friends in Berlin—and the strangers they dragged along. Eve was away on a ski trip in Switzerland with her rich friends, but Aria and her boyfriend, Paul, came. It was supposed to be a house party, but all parties in our house end up in my bedroom because it's the only place people can smoke and snort at the same time.

The Swede loved that Paul is a carpenter and told him how his biggest dream is to build his own boat one day. After the first hour, Paul had pronounced the Swede the Viking, and the Swede named him the Master. They left my bedroom and sat on the kitchen floor to talk—no, to scream—more comfortably about building a Viking ship and what it means to be a real man. Aria, Defne, and I danced on my bed all night, while Defne's friends kept taking more lines in a corner, Aria's friends made out like no one else was there, and Victor went to bed after the countdown.

Everyone else left to go to a bar around 3:00 a.m., but the Swede and I stayed in and fell asleep to the sound of fireworks exploding and bottles shattering on Skalitzer Strasse.

I woke up to Victor talking to a familiar voice outside my door. The Swede was sleeping soundly. I got out of bed, put my dress on, and stepped outside. It was Luka—a friend of mine and Victor's from my early party days who I hadn't seen in months. He looked like a ghost. A long-haired, skinny, amnesiac ghost.

We met him in a club three years ago and quickly found ourselves hanging out all the time. He was sleeping with my friend. I was sleeping with his. We would all meet in my room, wherever that was during that summer I kept changing rooms, do a bunch of cocaine, and have sex side by side. One time, though, when the boy I was sleeping with was not with us, I almost joined Julia and Luka. But anyway. This was over a year ago, which is a decade in Berlin time. We all stopped fucking each other soon after. I made the mistake of sleeping with the other boy one last time back in August, but that was it. Other than that, we're all friends now—or so I thought.

I went out and hugged Luka and said, "Happy New Year!" And he told me how he lost his wallet, keys, and all his friends dancing in Golden Gate. He left the club when he ran out of speed and had been walking aimlessly since, until he realized he was in front of our place and decided to ring our doorbell. His roommates were in a forty-eight-hour rave that he couldn't pay to get in and find them, so he couldn't go to his own place. Victor told him he could hang out with us until his roommates went home.

The Swede woke up and I introduced him to Luka. They looked at each other perplexed, trying to figure out what I could be doing with someone like the other. The Swede put his shirt on as Luka sat down on my couch. I told Luka that the Swede was visiting me for New Year's Eve but he was leaving soon to catch his flight, thinking it would be enough for Luka to leave the two of us alone, but he didn't seem to get the hint. Instead, he detailed which drugs he took, how high he was. The poor Swede packed his suitcase in silence.

I went into Victor's room, found him playing *Call of Duty* on his iMac, and asked him to come take Luka away.

When the Swede and I were left alone again, he turned to me and asked if I wanted to go to Sweden with him.

"I can't," I said. "I have to work."

"Then come whenever you have days off again," he said. "I'll buy your tickets and you won't have to spend money while you're there. Don't worry about any of that. I just want us to be together. Of course, if you want it too."

I said yes without even pretending to think about it.

When the Swede left, Luka came back into my room, asking if I wanted to watch something and try to sleep.

We got inside my bed and settled in on two ends of it, putting my laptop in the middle. I put on an episode of *Black Mirror* and fell asleep within the first five minutes. I dreamed of being out on Skalitzer Strasse. Someone told me that the sun had left Berlin, never to return again. I said,

"Okay, I don't mind. I will never stop loving this city." But I felt a horrifying pain in my head. Then I saw the Swede, and he held me, telling me the pain would pass. I woke up in the middle of the night with Luka's arms around me. I was holding his arms too. I turned around and realized it was him, and he was awake. I turned my back again, and moved to the edge of the bed, though it was hard to let go of the human warmth on a winter night.

"I'm sorry, Luka," I said. "I'm married now."

January 6

Gothenburg

It's been three days since I landed in Gothenburg, late at night. The Swede picked me up with his Volvo. The road to his apartment was dark and all the trees were covered in snow. He said I could put on any song I wanted, so I put on "If I Had a Heart." (He had never heard of Fever Ray before but knew the song from *Vikings*.)

He lives in a building in an area full of buildings identical to his, covered in snow. In the lobby of his building, there are flowers instead of graffiti like mine. In the elevator, there's music—not neighbors fighting, like in my staircase. He opened the door and waited for me to go in. No one in Berlin does that. He proudly showed me his Ikea kitchen, mountain-themed living room, cabin-like bedroom. Then he stood in front of a door and said, "And this is my dungeon. I hope it won't scare you away." He was talking about his little gaming closet.

He couldn't take the day off on such short notice, so he had to go to work the next morning. I woke up and had breakfast with him, watched him put on his suit, waited by the door until he got into the elevator. He was going to come back home for lunch, so I cleaned up the table, put the dishes in the dishwasher and the wine bottle we emptied in the recycling bag, made the bed, showered, brushed my teeth, put some of his fancy moisturizer on my body, talked to my mother and sister without telling them I was in Sweden, sent Eve, Aria, and Defne pictures of the Swede's apartment: the huge brown leather sofa and two moose antlers above it, the giant TV they all face and the shelf under it filled with books on how to make money—but also all the *Harry Potter* and *Lord of the Rings* DVDs, the empty boxes of snus and cigar that sit on his coffee table. The glass cabinet filled with model cars from the fifties, sixties, seventies. The other glass cabinet filled with whiskey and pictures of all the men in the Swede's family, hunting. (Except the Swede himself: he doesn't hunt.) (But he fishes.)

When he texted to let me know he was on his way, I microwaved the shepherd's pie he made before I arrived, set up the table, filled the pitcher with fresh water, turned off the soap I had been streaming in the background, and put on Swedish music from the sixties—not so much for him but for myself, since he only listens to American rock. I opened the door for him. We kissed. He took off his jacket and hung it up on the door of his gaming closet. We ate. I asked him about his morning. He said everyone at work now knew that I was here and wanted to meet me.

"Don't worry," he said. "I wouldn't do that to you."

He left quickly after he ate to be back at work on time. I put my soap back on, cleaned up the table, put the dishes in the dishwasher. I tried to write a short story about a middle-aged woman who gave up her adventurous life and married a stable and wealthy man. She didn't work and didn't paint like she once used to. She didn't have anything to do since the maid cleaned her big white house. All day she sat at her big white table and tried to write about her old days, but she couldn't. I couldn't.

In the evening, we went to the liquor store, which is called Systembolaget here, as in the system company. It's only open until 7:00 p.m. on weekdays and 10:30 a.m. on Saturdays, so all Swedes in suits rush to the nearest Systembolaget after work and fill their shopping carts with expensive, top-quality alcohol. I picked two bottles of red wine for us, one from Toscana and one pinot noir. Then we went to Ikea to buy a new duvet because the one he had made me sneeze and itch the first night. I told him he shouldn't, that I'd be fine, but he insisted. We ate meatballs at the food court.

All our days and nights passed like this. We cooked together, drove from one Swedish franchise to another, and watched movies lying below the antlers—well, he watched the movies I chose while I fell asleep ten minutes in.

And now back to real life I fly.

January 7

Berlin

It's Sunday morning. I'll go to work in a few hours. Defne had left my room when I arrived last night. She told me in a text that she's going to Turkey today to stay for six months. She's fleeing her roommate, her job, her nightmares to write her thesis in her parents' place.

Would I have gone back to my family if they'd stayed in my hometown, if I had a room with my high school diaries locked away in its drawers and Duman, Kurban, Depeche Mode posters on its walls? No, going back there would be worse than my aunt's couch. Who knows how many nights I spent in that room promising myself I would get out as soon as I hit eighteen and would never return. Teen Leyla would kill me if she knew I even thought about returning.

As if Defne's dramatic Turkish flight wasn't enough, I found out before I had my morning coffee that both of my roommates are moving out in the spring—Heidi forever, Victor for half a year. Victor will go to Barcelona for six months in May and Heidi will move to Wedding in April with her German friends who still have the energy to party every weekend. As a consolation gift for abandoning me, she gave me a KRZBRG T-shirt she got from the shop across the street and called me "really thug life, but in a good way." We waited for Victor to share with us the emotional motivation behind his decision or say something like "I'll miss you," but he didn't give us anything.

January 8

In my dream, everybody in my family was alive and happy. Both apartments I once lived in Istanbul were still mine. I had kept them both, paid their rents all these years in case I would want to go back one day. But now it was time to pack and move out. My mother, sister, and father all helped me put my belongings into boxes, but I woke up before I moved out of either of them.

January 9

Treasures of the day:

One box of peppermint tea

One bag of organic penne pasta

Arrabiata sauce (Why doesn't anyone leave any green pesto?)

One beer

Chips (open)

Milk (open)

I also found black Adidas sneakers on the street but they're not really my style, so I'll put them back where I found them tomorrow.

What do I want?

January 10

I like my job. I like my job. I like my job. I like my job.
I like my job. I like my job. I like my job. I like my job.
I like my job. I like my job. I like my job. I like my job.
I like my job. I like my job. I like my job. I like my job.
I like my job. I like my job. I like my job. I like my job.
I like my job. I like my job. I like my job. I like my job.
I like my job. I like my job. I like my job. I like my job.
I like my job. I like my job. I like my job. I like my job.
I like my job. I like my job. I like my job. I like my job.
I like my job. I like my job. I like my job. I like my job.

My flight to Gothenburg got delayed for an hour, so I'm sitting on the airport floor, rereading the first conversation Mona and I had in a year. I always thought I'd be colder if she ever got in touch with me again but seeing her name on my phone screen made me so happy I replied right away. After a couple of texts in which I summarized my life and she avoided telling me anything substantial about hers, Mona asked if I wanted to catch up on Skype. But I was already on my way to the airport, so I told her that.

"Where are you going?" she asked.

"I'm going to Sweden," I said. "Visiting a guy I met in a bar."

"Lol," she said, which read almost more abject than what she wrote next. "Milk him."

Milk him. What a nauseating idea. She must be on coke or drunk or both.

But why did *I* write back, "Haha, I'll try"?

She sent me a selfie she took using a glass-framed Nan Goldin self-portrait in the Getty as a mirror and wrote, "She makes me think of you!"

Mona's hair goes down to her shoulders now. She's wearing the high-waisted pleated skirt we'd bought together when she lived here. She had the same outfit on the day she first told me about her client who gave her the money to buy and wear it to their next appointment, the first tricks she'd ever turned, what "turning tricks" meant, as well as "johns" and some other words that sting in my mind to even think about right now, when I'm on my way to visit a man who paid for my ticket. I don't want to see the Swede as a john. He's not a john, right? I'm going to see him because I want to.

The Sky

"We could make a thousand in one hour if we met one of them together," she'd said on that Späti night in July after two bottles of wine and a couple of lines of ketamine in the bathroom. I'd laughed and dismissed her then as we walked to Sisyphos. The day she wore her pleated skirt. The day that came before the night of the failed coup. I was happy. Unconditionally happy. It was not because of the ketamine or the wine. It was because of the secret we now shared, the doors that Mona let me pass through and into her world by trusting me. I had never felt that close to anyone. Finally, I had found someone to surrender to. I wanted her to change me. I wanted to disappear in her, with her.

Slowly, she told me more about herself—or so I thought—and I believed that meant she was surrendering herself too. Her parents were both professors, yes, but that was not the full story. Her father had left Mona's mother when she was in high school, and her mother had been drunk ever since. She tried to kill herself once, while forcing Mona to sit across from her in the kitchen and watch. She swallowed a whole jar of pills, one by one, and drank the whole bottle of whiskey, but at the end, she slept like a pig and woke up like the pathetic woman she'd always been. As soon as she graduated from high school, Mona left her small town for Paris, where her father had a new life. But he didn't want anything to do with her. He only had enough love and money to give to his new young girlfriend.

Night by night, story by story, line by line, Mona and I got so close that I felt I didn't need anyone or anything else in life, except of course I did. I only had a couple hundred euros left in my negative bank account, and I didn't have a job. I'd stopped applying without realizing. I was not working on my thesis either. I was just sitting at home, eating pasta, and drinking cheap wine every day, watching Turkish TV on YouTube. Yes, I needed the money, and I was already using sex as a replacement for everything I couldn't have in life, including money. But that's not why I started working with Mona. I did it because I could only stand myself when I was with her.

There was nothing special about the night I said I wanted to go with her. She didn't make a big deal out of it, and I played along. We got undressed and took a photograph of the two of us together, naked, standing in front of the mirror. Two hours later, we met him at Hotel Adlon, where Michael Jackson once waved his baby over the balcony. The man said he was a lead singer in a band from Russia on tour. We figured he was telling the truth, considering the hotel we were at, the amount of coke he had on the table, and the outfit he was wearing. But we couldn't care less about who he was. We were high on our own lies. Mona told him she was twenty-five and from Montreal. I introduced myself as Cassandra, from Greece, also twenty-five.

Before we agreed to meet up with him, we'd said we wouldn't have sex with each other, only with him. He offered us an extra thousand to do it there. We said no right away. What we had was not to be reduced to sex for money—or worse—a man's pleasure. We both had sex with him but didn't touch one another. I actually came. But Mona didn't. Instead, she kept looking at me as they fucked with a childish victorious smile on her face that said, *Look at how easy it is to make him shake. How easy it is to make him moan. Isn't this fun?*

The idea that we could take back the money men made by exploiting us just like that was intoxicating, as if I were finding out that magic was real.

I remember how I kept checking if the 500-euro note was in my purse. That one note, earned in less than one hour, was enough to pay one month's rent and utilities. I had next month's rent covered, I was high on coke, my favorite person was with me. I was content. But the bleach I feared splashed on to me as soon as Mona got off the train to go to her place. What if my mother found out? What if my sister found out? What if the whole country found out? And what if I got caught? Sex work was technically not a crime in Germany, but people got arrested for practicing it on their own terms. If I got caught, I would have been deported within hours. Worse, the Turkish government would know why I'd been deported. Who knows what they'd do with that kind of information.

But I still met more men with Mona after the Russian Michael Jackson because when she was with me, there was no room for fear or remorse. Her freedom used to set me free as well.

After each date, we'd treat ourselves to a festive dinner or breakfast at places in deep West Berlin, where no one knew us. We'd talk about how our capitalist countries raised us to be proud of making money, made it completely normal to profit off of our sexuality, but they both drew a line when it came to women profiting from their own sexuality. In France, it seemed, capitalism allowed feminism to evolve up to the point where women saw that nothing bad happened when they had sex with men they chose or when they made money doing anything but. They raised the barricades at the checkpoint where women would see they could have sex with men they chose and make money doing it.

In Turkey, I explained to Mona, most people viewed sex workers as fallen women whose lives had been irrevocably ruined by sins, whether it was the women or their abusers who committed them. And women who had sex outside of marriage were seen as whores, whether they asked for money or not. Only the women who remained with their abusers or married one of their clients deserved respect from society. Only they were holy.

Sex workers had to carry the weight of everyone's sins in Turkey: the capitalists, the patriarchs, the bitter matriarchs.

In Turkey, we've all become numb to news stories about sex workers being raped, murdered, and thrown out of speeding cars on dark side streets. But we love watching scenes in movies and soap operas about them: a single mother whose husband started selling her against her will when she was young and beautiful, for example. Who knows how many characters like this I've seen on TV growing up: a choiceless woman who either got murdered by a client or saved by marrying one, who then kept her to himself in the end.

Capitalism used every TV channel, news story, and institution to indoctrinate its subjects to internalize that sex and money were the ultimate prizes for their services but kept it a crime to have sex for money, because if subjects had access to gaining both, why would they keep serving their exploiters? It was okay to forgive a woman who'd been forced to have sex for money, but a woman who did it by choice was an irredeemable threat to society.

How did they trick us into believing it was more honorable to work as a clerk to old rich men, a saleswoman of child-labored toys, or a waitress for minimum wage and then go home to perform the perfect mixture of strong and sweet femininity to our partners and families? How did they trick us into believing we had to earn our equality by beating men at their own game, and they owed us nothing, after centuries of being held captive in homes, forced to do all sorts of domestic labor for free?

What's so sacramental about sex? If our bodies are so sacred, then why is it okay to use it to clean for others, cook, carry, build for others for money so little it barely pays for our rents? If our honor is so important, then why is it okay to let corporate managers insult it as they please?

It felt like Mona took the answers to all these questions with her when she left.

I had not told anyone about how I paid for rent those couple of months—except for Victor, who was almost a little too excited about the idea that I could get rich. (And equally disappointed when I stopped.) (Neither his communist upbringing nor capitalist aspirations helped him understand how commodification of one's sexuality could paralyze them socially and economically, like it did to me.) (Even though I did it willingly.) (Sometimes the things we do willingly hurt us the most.) (Most of the time, really.) I barely saw anyone anyway.

But after Mona left and I submitted my thesis (which I'd postponed writing as long as I could and barely put together at the last minute while spending the little money I saved, trying to find a new job, and watching the news from Turkey) to the university, I began meeting old friends again. It felt like the necessary thing to do. Aria had started seeing Paul and hanging out with a group of pretentious poets who seemed to be only capable of talking about

Walt Whitman and David Foster Wallace—although I never heard anything come out of their mouths to indicate they've actually read their writing. Heidi always hung out with a German group who didn't speak much English. Victor was too busy with work. They all tried making space for me in their lives again, but I felt like I didn't fit in. Once or twice, Aria asked what happened to me.

"You're not the same Leyla," she said.

I said it was the attempted coup, my approaching graduation, being stuck in my writing. I said being in Berlin didn't protect me from myself anymore. I was finally disenchanted.

Aria didn't buy it, but she didn't press me on it either. This is why I loved living in Berlin, where privacy was a right that didn't make you feel like you're betraying your community by practicing it. If I were in Istanbul, I knew, my friends wouldn't stop asking until they found out the truth, let alone my family.

Since Mona'd left, whenever the thought of those men that paid us for sex came to my mind, I successfully swept it under the rug. A third-person soap opera narrator could suggest I became so good at sweeping away that life, it turned me into a professional cleaner. I barely thought of those days at all in the last months. And of course, that's exactly why Mona had to resurface now, bringing all these questions with her.

The plane is about to land in Gothenburg. The Swede must be waiting for me at the airport, feeling all sorts of naive and pure emotions. And here I am, asking myself if

The Applicant

I'm here because the Swede is a socially acceptable john, and I am only capable of enjoying a man's company if they pay me in some way. Am I forever broken or only temporarily thrown off by Mona again? Or was Mona texting me today of all days a sign—a reminder from Cassandra that no man is worthy of sharing my true self or emotions?

January 14

Auf der Autobahn

As soon as he picked me up from the airport, the Swede asked if I wanted to go on a road trip. He took Monday off, so we could drive to wherever I wanted.

The last time I was here, we had tried to make a list of things we both liked to do. Road trips were one of the five things we could come up with, unless we opened up eating and drinking and gave every meal and drink its own number on the list. The others were smoking cigars and traveling.

We decided to go to Malmö to see my old roommate Erik, who invited us to a posh house party. He said the host was a friend of a friend of a friend. All night, Erik was running around the flat from one toilet to the other with his gang, in his fedora and his tropical shirt, yet nobody else in the party seemed to see them. He used to work as a cleaner, too, when we lived together in Neukölln and I worked for the startup. We were already having the same conversations we had on this visit in club gardens then, over and over again. Erik works in a big company as a marketing associate now and earns over 30,000 Swedish kronur. He hates his life.

I told two guys who were kind of flirting with me on the balcony that I'm a cleaner. They said it was too cold and went back inside.

I found the Swede, who was talking to a stranger about whiskey and cigars and told him I was bored.

"Let's go then," he said.

"But Erik doesn't look like he wants to leave anytime soon," I said. We were supposed to stay at his place.

The Swede took out his phone and booked us a hotel room. I tried to stop him. I didn't want him to spend more money on this trip. That's why I chose to come to Malmö, where we could stay with Erik and I could avoid using "hotel rooms" and "the Swede" in the same sentence after everything I wrote on the flight here. But he wouldn't listen to me.

"Am I your early midlife crisis sports car?" I asked him in the taxi.

He laughed and said, "I hope so. Otherwise I'll be screwed when you get bored of me."

It wasn't even midnight when we got into our hotel room, but we both fell asleep right away. We woke up with the hard knocks on our door and a voice: "Housekeeping!"

I thought for a second that I had fallen asleep at work, at Looking Glass, and it was all a dream. Then, I remembered the dream I'd just woken from, in which Mona and a stranger were in bed with me instead of the Swede. But when I opened my eyes, there he was, the sleeping Swede, holding me tight, leaving no room to doubt whether he was a john or not. Being with the Swede was the opposite of being at work. It felt like eating a meal my mother cooked, swimming in the Mediterranean, or walking in Beyoğlu.

We're driving back home now. I mean Gothenburg.

January 21

Berlin

Back in Kreuzberg. I was supposed to come back four days ago and work through the weekend, but on the morning of my flight, when I woke up next to the Swede in Gothenburg and realized that I was holding him with a sort of strength I never thought I had, I asked if I should stay a little longer.

He said yes without thinking. We let the return ticket go and booked a new one for Sunday, today.

The Swede told me he loves me—and not during sex or right before he flew across an international border. He said it when we were making Swedish meatballs in his kitchen and our hands were buried in minced meat and onions.

"You don't have to say it back," he said.

At first I didn't. But then I did.

"This doesn't mean we're in a relationship," I said.

"But if we love each other, why try to hide it?"

We didn't say anything else for a while. But from that moment on, we kept saying "love you" to each other at every excuse: before he went to work, when he came back for lunch, before he left for work again, when he came back home, before we went to sleep. I thought we both kept saying it to stock up on "I love you's" until I left and we both returned to our real lives. But he already booked his flights to come to Berlin in two weeks and now I'm stuck with these yucky words, *II lovvve yyou*, these distasteful words, which there's no use in denying that I feel, even though it makes my life sound like a rom-com. Not even a soap, since I can't say them in Turkish to the Swede. So maybe it doesn't count.

January 26

I only had nine checkouts on my list today so most of the time I pretended to work. I didn't find anything except a few bottles I could have returned for Pfand, but I left them since I work tomorrow, too, and I hope to find more. We're not allowed to store our bottles at the hostel. They say there's not enough space, so we all have our own secret locations to hide them. (I put mine under the stairs of the 100s, left corner.)

After work, I went to Wedding to see Aria. I brought wine and she cooked a vegan dinner. We talked about boys all night: old, new, and hypothetical. Aria was thrilled when she heard me say "me too" to the Swede on the phone.

"You have a boyfriend!" she yelled. "Finally I can talk to someone about being in love and happy."

I tried to convince her that I don't have a boyfriend and I'm not sure what happiness or love is supposed to feel like, but she couldn't stop talking about what bliss it is to be with a man who isn't a Berlin dick, who doesn't use being an artist as an excuse to be a selfish asshole.

I left when Paul came home from the workshop. Walking to the U-Bahn, I thought about how our lives *look* so different than couples in soaps or the cautionary tales of feminist movies from the seventies. But is it really? All my girlfriends only socialize when their boyfriends are away doing their own thing and when we are together all they want to talk about is their relationships.

On the U-Bahn, I got off at the wrong stop in a panic, thinking it was my stop and afraid of missing it, and I broke my phone's screen.

What do I have left? What do I have that I like and can keep? What do I want that I can get and won't turn me into a Thérèse Chevalier, a Jeanne Dielman, my mother?

January 27

Some nice things about my job to remember before I go to work in an hour:

1. For lunch, we can eat what we serve guests for breakfast. Most of my colleagues bring healthy meals from home, but I always eat the same combination of free food: a white Brötchen cut into two. Two slices of salami, one pink with pistachio and one dark brown. I place one piece on each side of the Brötchen. I take one slice of breakfast cheese, cut it into two, and cover the salami Brötchens with them. I warm the sandwiches up in the oven for a few minutes and put them on a plate next to each other and above a banana, which makes the sandwiches the two-colored eyes of a smiley face.

2. I can't think of anything else now. Got to go.

My sister accuses me of ruining her life by leaving our mother to her care, as if she were sick or needed special care. My mother says it's my sister who needs *her*.

Before I blocked her number, my sister sent me a hundred messages about how stuck she feels, how selfish I am, how I don't deserve to be her sister, how she couldn't recognize me anymore, how our mother would die of loneliness if she stopped living with her, and how it would be my fault.

This cycle repeats itself at least once a year, and I'm not sure if I can take it any longer. I wish I could help them, but I can't. I couldn't pull them out of their depression even if I lived in Turkey. True, I could have tried harder to have an advertising career in Turkey or written a steel-plated thesis here, but I can't change who I am—or the past. True, I could go back now, call all my connections, take any job I can find, and move in with them. But then I would turn into my sister. I would be worse. All the anger I've been avoiding since I left would resurface, and I would blame them for everything.

The only reason they live together is that they both want to. They could part ways in a month if they really wanted. My mother could try to find a job for once in her life and my sister could take an extra job. They're stuck together because they choose to be. And I choose to live as far away from them as possible, even if it means I have to clean bathrooms, stairs, the rooms of strangers. Why should I feel guilty about it and not them?

When my father died, I lost my enemy, but my sister lost her hero. Nothing he did lessened her love for him. Then again, I never met the version of my parents my sister knew before I was born. My sister moved away for college when I was seven, and I grew up with a man who took pride in being frightening. Not only to us but also to his employees, servers, or people he'd threaten in traffic fights.

But he wasn't always a villain. Some days, he charmed everyone with his attentive questions, genuine laughs, green eyes. Some nights, he'd come home with flowers for my mother or my favorite chocolate cake. He'd hug and kiss me on both cheeks, then sniff my hair and say, "Ohh, mis kızım benim." As a child, I always hugged him back. But as years went by, his sympathetic days made his violent episodes harder to endure. I joined my mother in her fear at home and embarrassment when he flared up in front of others. Even though I, too, was beginning to blow up at those who were the closest to me, just like him and my sister.

Would my sister have ever stopped copying our father's hurtful outbursts if she'd seen his desperation that night, after he crashed into that innocent man's car, driving drunk?

I was seventeen when I opened the door to the police. I was the one to see him in bruises for the first time. I was alone when my mother told me that my father had killed a father of five. My sister was in another city, where she'd been for a decade. When my father went to prison, she moved back home to take care of his business, but this time it was my turn to go away for college. We were bound from the beginning to play the same role in the same tragedy, always on different stages.

Last night, I went to Eve's to share the half-full bottle of Hendrick's I found at work. We skipped dinner and went straight to gin and cigarettes.

I told Eve about my sister. How she took her anger toward her own life out on me again. Eve told me about her own mother. How she often did the same. When Eve was in college, she got pregnant after a one-night stand. She was still religious at the time and so was her mother. Abortion was taboo in their small town, but her mother made her get one anyway. "A child will ruin your life," she said. "Look at me, my life. I could have been a doctor if I didn't have you. Or a lawyer. I could have found love." Eve knew it was the right thing to do, but it didn't stop her from feeling sinful for years. Disgraceful. Deep down, she said, she never stopped being ashamed. And neither did her mother. That's why living together was torture for them both. They reminded each other of their shared disgrace.

On the way to the Späti to buy more gin, Eve held my hands, crossed them with hers, and started playing the spinning game in the middle of Rosa Luxemburg Platz. We laughed, we screamed, we spinned intensely, as if we were two kids free-falling down a time tunnel in a cartoon from the nineties and not two grown-up foreigners drifting in Berlin. Then, Eve fell. I don't remember how it happened since we were already drunk, but she said I let her go. Her lips were bleeding and she kept saying how much her ribs were hurting. She kept blaming me all night, and I kept apologizing. In the end, my apologies turned into apologies to my sister, apologies I never gave. Apologies for letting her go like she said I did.

In my dream, I visited my sister and mother in Turkey. They were begging for money on the streets, but they took me to Beyti afterward, an expensive restaurant in Istanbul where we used to go in my childhood. The kebab was perfect, just the right amount of juice and spice. I can still taste all of its flavors in my mouth. But I never asked for it. I never asked to be held. I didn't want to spin. I only want to be. Away.

January 30

It's the middle of the night. I woke up and I can't go back to sleep. I'm meeting the director of my department tomorrow.

January 31

I woke up five minutes before the alarm went off. I drank green tea instead of coffee. I put on my dress. I brushed my teeth and my hair. I put concealer under my eyes and light pink lipstick on, to look more like a good girl, a model student eager to continue her studies. I left twenty minutes earlier than I had to. It had been over six months since I last went to the university and I thought I could get lost on the way because of that. But nothing had changed about the route. Nothing had changed about the main building.

Except for the doors. I could swear you had to pull them open last year. I pulled and pulled, but the doors didn't open. Then, a tiny blond girl ten years younger than me pushed it gently, and there I was, inside one of the oldest universities in Europe, which I was suing. *This is a sign, a reminder. I'll go in there with a smile on my face and explain myself calmly*, I thought. *They'll understand me this time.* After making two rounds on floors of the building other than my department's, I finally went into the hallway where the offices of my old professors were located. I walked as fast as I could so I wouldn't have to see the one who failed me. But the director had other plans for our meeting.

He made me wait in front of his door for twenty minutes. Twenty minutes! In Germany! I didn't run into anyone I knew, which made me think that they all knew I was coming and didn't leave their offices on purpose. When he finally let me in, he told me to sit on the couch. Another old man was sitting on a chair by the couch. He was their lawyer.

"I didn't know we were supposed to bring lawyers," I said.

"We weren't, don't worry, he's here to take notes," the director said.

It's not like I had a lawyer to bring. I was all alone in this appeal. Heidi and Google Translate were my only help (not exactly even paralegals). But it made me uneasy from the beginning to think that their version of this meeting would go to the court.

The director took his time to leave his desk and come to the sitting area and when he finally did, he sat across me, put one leg on top of the other, and stretched his arms on each side of the couch.

He said, "So?"

I said, "So."

I heard in a soap once that you should never be the first one to speak in a negotiation. But it wasn't a negotiation. They made it clear right away that they weren't going to reevaluate my thesis or give me a chance to write another one. They said it would be against the university's quality standards and principles.

What principles? The professor who failed me has been reading the same lectures from his decades-old book for years. Students have been complaining about his teaching skills since the beginning of his career. Another professor told us so. I chose him as my adviser because the year above us said he passed everyone without reading their whole theses. He let all my friends pass with sloppy theses but when it came to me (the odd Turkish student who insisted on writing a protean thesis about Turkish immigrants in Germany) all of a sudden he had standards. Most professors have been giving the same tests to every class since the program started. We all cheated on all our finals. Is sitting there like that in front of a student you made wait for twenty minutes standing outside your door also a principle? These were my thoughts, but I couldn't say them without burning all bridges. I thought about writing a story about a student who gets kicked out of the university and decides to blow up the building. I also thought about kicking the director in the balls.

He asked why I didn't just get a work visa.

I explained to him that without graduating from the program, I'm not eligible to get a job-seeking visa, which is the only visa that allows Turks to work more than twenty hours a week, in any job they want. A work visa is only granted to those who get offers for full-time jobs directly related to their field of study and that pays more than net 2,500 euros a month. No company in Berlin would hire an English major from Turkey with that as a starting salary. Without a job-seeking visa, a work visa, or a student visa, I cannot stay here.

He asked why I didn't apply to become a refugee.

What he meant was, I either had to be the perfect student or a poor refugee to have a seat in the auditoriums of his country's conscientious institutions. The middle seats were all reserved for people who looked like him.

I had to try hard not to cry.

He gave me a German "sorry" and repeated how they all agreed that they would not change their decision to fail me unless the court orders them to.

"If you had made that decision already, why did you invite me here?" I asked.

"Because the court advised so," he said.

I told them I'd see them at the hearing and went to work. I cleaned sixteen rooms, six bathrooms, and one kitchen.

I sprayed and wiped. I vacuumed and dusted. I counted the copper coins I found under the beds and put them in my pocket—like how thousands of people who looked like me had done for decades. For decades, we scrubbed their toilets, worked in their factories, built their classrooms so they could keep their kids segregated from ours. All the while, people who looked like them went to schools, stayed focused, traveled abroad for a taste of the exotic, came back, announced themselves open-minded, progressive. They got their MAs and PhDs. They participated in academia exactly the way they were told to, with the peace of mind knowing that it was a system that was founded to serve them. They kept their ideas sterile, within the limits of the mainstream ideologies of their country.

While we cleaned, cooked, served, they thought, wrote, framed. Their government paid them stipends from birth through college. They boasted about their independent TV, their welcoming democracy, their genetic efficiency, while we bowed our heads at the mention of our corrupt media, our autocratic history, our conservative upbringing. They wrote and reviewed papers, theses, and dissertations with the confidence of a Western intellectual in countries where intellectuality was rewarded and not punished. They proudly called themselves perfectionists, never seeing the flaw in expecting everyone to be "perfectly" aligned with their expectations of right and wrong.

Of course these people won't realize that kicking someone out of the university can ruin their life in the ways that it's ruining mine. They don't know what real life is. So obsessed with academic integrity, they fail to comprehend what human integrity is. It's more important for them to perform perfection in their fields than to give a second chance to someone begging for one.

This is the same logic that doesn't let refugees cross borders in the US or Switzerland or Japan, simply because they don't have all the *documents*. This is the logic that runs and ruins the world. How stupid I was to believe that academia was ever interested in doing any good! No wonder I failed. I really didn't understand the way the world worked.

The hierarchy of writing serves the hierarchy of borders. Universities are above and beyond border patrol headquarters. Professors are its gatekeepers.

February 1

Treasures of the day:
Cauliflower
Garlic
Onion
Half a pumpkin

The food was in a plastic bag in the fridge of the common kitchen, labeled with the guest-departure date of four days ago, but then there was another note written by someone from the staff who cleaned that floor two days before me. It said, "Please correct the departure dates on your food, otherwise the team will have to take it." I took it, but I feel guilty. Did yesterday's cleaner know that the bag belongs to a guest who has extended their stay? Were they just too lazy to label them again? Was I stealing the food? But if I didn't take the food and the head of the maids came to check on me, she would be upset I didn't get rid of it when the departure date had passed.

The disquiet followed me all the way home.

My Fiktionsbescheinigung expires on June 14. If the university had told me they wouldn't change their decision instead of making me wait one and a half months for a meeting, I may have had a hearing date already. Now, I only have four and a half months left. Heidi and I wrote the court a new letter today to request an expedited hearing or verdict. But Germans hate being rushed. What if my request peeves the clerk who opens the letter? Could he take longer than he would have to move forward with my case?

February 5

I just walked the Swede to the U-Bahn.

We decided to see each other every other week. It will cost him a lot of money, but he says he doesn't mind as long as we can be together.

"I have this strong urge to take care of you," he said before he left.

"That's the voice of capitalist patriarchy," I said to him. "But you can try if you want."

February 14

I've been down with the flu since yesterday, but yesterday I worked anyway, because they only pay half when you don't show up to work whether you get a sick note or not. It was not easy to climb up and down the bunk beds. Alessio helped me out. He's this Italian cleaner who might be a misguided angel in dreadlocks. Dreadlock to be precise. He only has one long lock; the rest of his hair is shaved. He was a construction worker before this job so he can finish all his tasks in the first half of his shift, and he spends the rest of the day helping others.

After work, I met Eve at a bar that she wanted me to check out for the reading. She said she'd met the owners at a party, and they seemed like exactly the people I'd been looking for. I went, and even though I had a sore throat I had a drink and smoked a cigarette. I was in a good mood because I had just received forty red roses from the Swede, with a card signed: *Yours*.

On the U8 a hot saxophone player looked at me and said, "One last song for the beautiful lady," or I imagined that he looked at me because I was still under the influence of the roses. And maybe he wasn't that handsome.

A talented street musician would be a perfect match for me. I pictured the two of us outside the U8, in a park, but I couldn't imagine myself kissing him. The Swede is my complete opposite, but I can't keep my hands off him when he's around.

I'm scared of finding out who I would be without my job and the Swede now. This is insane and an exaggeration. Too much television wrote that.

The bar is on Sonnenallee, called Atwood, and owned by a French Canadian couple: Eloise and Annie. Eve truly came through this time. Eloise is a painter and Annie is a writer. Both are in their thirties I think. They gave me a warm welcome and a mezcal cocktail on the house. I read them the first page of my diary. They both said they loved it and asked if I wanted to have the reading in ten days. I said yes, of course.

As soon as I got home, I started typing up what I wrote on these pages in August and September. I stayed up until 5:00 a.m. transcribing my life in fragments.

I saved the document as "The Applicant."

February 18

I'm on my way to the airport because the Swede is on his way to Berlin. I can't believe I turned into one of those people who go to the airport to pick someone up with public transportation.

Ali cried today, after lunch. He said he's been crying a lot since he started this job. Then he confessed that he didn't tell the new guy he's been seeing he is a cleaner because he felt that his being a cleaner was what made the other Tinder dates disappear. He said the guy's ex is a hot dancer and Ali himself is just a cleaner and some other things as we stood in the hallway with mops in our hands until he stopped sobbing and we went back to cleaning. We scrubbed sinks, we unclogged toilets, we changed bedsheets, we vacuumed traveler's hairs off the floor, we dried the mirrors perfectly so that the party people can make themselves up. We finished. We sat at the bar and talked about visas, money, and boys until we finished our free beers too.

Then I returned my bottles and went home.

I unblocked and called my sister, who had been sending messages through my mother for weeks now, apologizing for what she said. If I could help Ali feel better, if I could accept Eve for who she is, I could be a better sister too. We talked for an hour. She told me about the jobs she's been applying for, how she's going to rent a three-bedroom apartment as soon as she gets one of them so I'd have my own room when I visit. How much she loved me and our mother and how I shouldn't take her seriously when she complained. That these arguments happened in every family. I told her I didn't think so, but she laughed and said they did, they did.

"Hadi biraz da sen anlat, kara kutu seni," she teased me. So I told her about the reading I'm getting ready for, the people at work, and the Swede. She asked if I was happy. I said yes. I think I am.

February 23

The reading was a full house, at least fifty people were in the audience. Only a few of them were my guests: Heidi, Victor, Aria, Ash, and Yvonne. The rest were Eve's friends and the bar's regulars. Eloise said I could drink as much as I wanted, so I got drunk before people started coming in. I remember reading, leaving the bar, buying a kebab and a pack of cigarettes with the confidence of the 50 euros I made, and falling down the stairs of the U-Bahn.

I'm okay though. I made it home in one piece and with just one small bruise on my knee.

In the morning, Heidi and Victor started filling me in on the details of the night that I didn't remember, but I had to stop them because every word that came out of their mouths turned into an embarrassing scene on TV in my mind that made me want to zap the channel or leave the room—except that wouldn't help since I was the TV screen.

I ate all the Brötchen I could stomach to kick the hangover and went back to work. But the scenes from last night didn't leave me alone there either. I cleaned one mirror maybe five times over while I was thinking about how I threw each page I was done reading on the ground, what Yvonne—the ex-ambassador of class and healthy living—might have thought about my performance, and how the word Fiktionsbescheinigung resisted coming out of my mouth, but I didn't get the hint and tried until people from the audience said it for me.

If this were any other city, my performance could have cost me my nonexistent writing career. But it seems like it earned me one in Berlin. Eve texted me saying everyone loved the reading and wanted to throw a dinner party in my honor on Sunday. I hope I'll find a couple of good bottles while cleaning to take there.

After work, I decided to submit what I read at the reading to a journal. I hadn't submitted anything to any journals in a year, since that time when I tried and got rejected by all of them. I googled "literary journals that pay." I sent my diary excerpt as I edited it for the reading to a magazine on top of the list. They ask for no cover fee and they pay $300 per story, so why not? I'll probably get a rejection letter in six months and have another reason to drink.

Then Ash stopped by with his new friend Colin from Romeo before they went to a party in About Blank. Colin is fifty-seven and he just moved to Berlin from New York. He's convinced this is the best place to live. "So cheap, so artsy." He's volunteering at an art gallery until he finds a job. I couldn't tell him that he'll be volunteering forever if he wants to work in galleries in Berlin. Instead, I kept filling his glass with wine as we sat on the floor and listened to *The Velvet Underground & Nico*. When we were out of wine, they offered me poppers. We closed our eyes and lay in bed. When I opened my eyes, they were gone.

It's 2:00 a.m. I'm tired and a little drunk. I don't have to work tomorrow, and I don't want to sleep, but I can't afford to do anything other than to listen to "All Tomorrow's Parties" on repeat.

February 24

I woke up on the couch today, so thirsty from all the wine and poppers I barely made it to the coffee machine. I found my phone on the floor under the couch. There were ten missed calls from my mother and two texts from the Swede, fiftysomething WhatsApp notifications from a group chat about the dinner party at Eve's. It took me a while to remember to refresh my emails. But when I did, I saw an email from the editor of the journal I sent my diary to last night. She wanted to know if it was all real. She only had space in the memoir section, and she had to make sure it was actually about my life.

I replied immediately. "Yes! I just changed people's genders, ages, names, nationalities. But other than that, it's all real."

Half an hour later, I remembered I didn't change anything about myself in the piece. My failures at cleaning, having sex in Sisyphos, my drug use. Do I want them to appear in print as a memoir?

There was a time when my biggest dream was to become a journalist. Then, I realized I've been given fiction as facts by newspapers, governments, history, friends, and my family all my life. I thought I'd surrendered to fiction a long time ago. I've sent out fiction stories to dozens of literary journals and I never even got a personalized rejection. Now, all I did was put the feelings on paper next to the events that caused them, and everybody loved it.

I called my sister to ask for advice.

"Should I use a pseudonym?"

She said yes immediately, without a trace of doubt in her voice, which made me want to do the exact opposite.

"Of course you'd say that," I said. Then I hung up on her.

I imagined myself teaching literature at a university in Turkey, telling my students to challenge all forms of authority, making them read writers who rebelled against their dictators and outlived them in their afterlives. I saw myself getting fired, maybe arrested if I was famous enough, for promoting drug use. I could see news articles about me being a junkie, a whore anyway. What did I know about activism? What could that girl who spent years in Berlin fucking and snorting when the country was going through so much know about justice?

Then I thought, no. I'm just being paranoid because of my genes and all the weed I smoked in college. Let's hope I'll never have to find out. Or is this drama what I really want? What's the source of this fear: growing up watching my country's most-read writers go to court for things their fictional characters said, or do I owe it all to my mother?

It's too late for the past now. Recovering the past in memory is an impossible task. Memory is fiction constantly rewriting itself. Fiction is the only source I can rely on to write a memoir and apparently calling it nonfiction is the easiest way to publish fiction.

But these philosophical investigations will be useless if I get kicked out of Europe in a few months and have to move back to Turkey.

I texted my sister a red heart.

February 25

Last night, I put on my dress, indulged myself with a 5-euro bottle of wine and a discounted 3-euro box of Guylian chocolates, and walked all the way to Rosa Luxemburg Platz for the dinner at Eve's. We were eight in total, but I only knew Eve, Aria, Eloise, and Annie. I'd briefly met the others at the reading, but they welcomed me as though we've been friends for months. I wasn't sure if it was because they heard me read fifteen pages from my diary or because I'd spent more time at their table than I remembered that night.

One of them was a quiet German writer in her late thirties, Judith, who'd lived in London for a decade and just moved back to Berlin. She had an acquired but fitting Britishness in the way she spoke, listened to others, and held her glass. Then there was Annika, a Russian-turned-German citizen around Eve's age. She had short, Barbie-blond hair and a stabilized cynicism in her voice. And next to Annika sat the bartender at Atwood, a twenty-four-year-old Bavarian named Malte, who went to school for law but decided to become a theater actor instead.

They were all creative, beautiful, classy. In the beginning, I felt fresh, too, the way I'd feel on the first day of a school or job I was excited about—or when I was new to Berlin. Even my dress looked new to me in the mirror of Eve's bathroom. I looked at my hand holding Eve's wineglass and for a second it felt like it was someone else's hand. I sounded different when I was speaking to Judith about Rachel Cusk, as if I had lived in London for a decade and acquired a British calm. I had something to say about every subject, like I had always been one of them. I told them about my journal acceptance and regretted it immediately since it's not confirmed yet, but it was already too late, so I shared every single detail of my correspondence with the editor.

The food had olives and sour cream all over it and even being this poor doesn't stop me from being picky with food, so I was already tipsy with two glasses of wine. The drunker I got, the more put together everyone seemed to me, against myself. Aria, who always complains about how she can't stand Berlin's creative socialites, looked like she was there as one of them and not my plus one. Eve, who normally can't stop talking about men in her life, now only told others about the new Vietnamese bar on her street, the most recent gallery opening she attended, the last Lars von Trier film she saw, as if she were giving an interview in front of an audience and not talking with friends in her own home. It made me feel like I was being observed too. I didn't want to speak anymore. I didn't know where to look or what to do with my hands other than checking my phone. I saw that my mother had called me five times so I stepped outside the room to call her back. Of course, it wasn't an emergency at all. She wanted to remind me to watch the new episode of *Uzak*. I told her I was out and went back to the table.

Annika asked what was wrong and I told everyone how I have to get back to my family's phone calls before too long no matter where I am or what I may be doing.

"Is it a Turkish thing?" Annika asked.

"I'm pretty sure we're a special case even for Turkey," I told them.

When I was in college in Istanbul, I spent months following an avant-garde theater group all around the city as their unpaid assistant director. I used to live in a three-bedroom apartment all by myself, so we would all come back to my place after rehearsal, drink until noon the next day discussing *The Myth of Sisyphus*, sleep, wake up, rehearse, do it all again. One day, we all woke up with an endless buzz and loud knocks on the door. It was the security guard of the residence I lived in. My father, who could not reach me, called security and asked them to check on me. I checked my phone and saw over twenty missed calls from my father. I was mortified. I called my father and asked why we had to talk five times a day. Maybe I wanted the theater people to hear I was rebelling against authority and surveillance like a good avant-garde. I told my father that I was twenty-one and everyone around me only talked to their families once a week. We didn't have anything to talk about, so why couldn't he leave me alone for one damn day? At first, he was silent, then he said that we weren't like other families. They loved me too much not to hear my voice for a whole day. My mother uses the same guilt-trip tricks I told them, so the easiest thing is to just give her what she wants.

"Next time your father calls, you should tell him it's time for him to die and set you free," Annika said. "Send him that essay, 'The Death of the Father.' Who was it by? Freud? Barthes?"

"The Death of the Author," I said.

"What?"

"Nothing. My father actually died that summer."

After a moment of funereal silence, Eloise and Annie asked if I wanted to turn the diary readings into a monthly show. I said yes, people cheered and toasted, and then I left. I didn't want them to see me get drunker and change their minds. And I didn't want to be there not drunker any longer and change mine.

Eve walked me to the door and said, "These people are at the very top of Berlin's literary scene, and they all love your writing. Don't you think it's magical that your piece got accepted on the same day? Your luck is finally turning around, Leyla, I can feel it."

Walking down the stairs, I thought that if my time in Berlin wasn't running out, if I at least had a hearing set up, I could have been as excited as Eve. It's draining to play the hopeful appellant when the court hasn't responded to the request I made over three weeks ago.

If I had a little more time on my visa to stay here or at least outside of Turkey, this could have been the start of my big break. It's always how it goes for young writers in movies and novels. But my life is not an American movie or a European novel. It's not up to the Turkish cleaner on a visa to overcome all obstacles between herself and what she desires. It's up to Ausländerbehörde officers, court clerks, and university professors to let her stay so she can do it. And they won't, because they're the cleaners of their own stories, and clearly they're better heroines than I am. How seamlessly they shake off the unruly student from their perfect institutions, rinse the country off the defeated, send the unworthy down the sink. They're naturals at this.

All the way back home from Eve's, I talked to the Swede on the phone. He said he was so proud when he heard about my acceptance that he told his whole family about it at dinner, and now they all wanted to read the excerpt, including the Swede. Hearing the word "proud" made all the guilt of disappointing my mother and sister come back to me. It made me feel dirty.

"I don't think you'd want that," I said. "It's mostly about drugs and sex with the guy I was seeing before you."

"Understood," he said, laughing one of his giant laughs.

I asked him if he'd be okay with me reading what I wrote about him next month.

"I'd love that," he said.

"But you don't know what I wrote about you."

"I trust you."

"I'm not so sure if you should," I said.

"Me neither," he said. "But I do."

I left the Swede's apartment only two times in the last four days. Once for the store and once to meet his best friend, Lars, who lives just around the corner.

Lars and his wife, Linnea, live in an apartment identical to the Swede's in size and shape. They also have the same couch in black, same TV, same plates, and same candles that they've put on the same plate in the same impractical way that makes the candles melt into each other. (But who is to say we are any better in Berlin, sticking Aldi candles on Lidl wine bottles, thinking we each live the most original life under our high ceilings.)

The Swede and Lars are the kind of friends who show their affection by making fun of each other as though they're in a tennis match, hard and fast. You'd think they'd know each other well after a decade of best friendship, but the Swede was hearing about Lars's family story with me for the first time.

Lars's mother was a hippie who left him and his two brothers to their father and ran off with another hippie. His father was an engineer who often taught the kids the wrong things, like which hand to hold cutlery with or how to put on a shirt.

Linnea, Lars, and the Swede all met each other working at Volvo, although now Linnea and Lars were back in school: Linnea to become a social worker and Lars to learn web design.

"Lars is the most talented salesman I know," said the Swede. "It took him ten years, but he even managed to get Linnea to marry him." The giant's laughter followed.

Lars responded without losing any time, congratulating the Swede for tricking me into a relationship. I joined Lars's side. We teased the Swede about his politics. I usually avoid talking to the Swede about politics, but Lars was great at roasting him. He told me that the Swede is the only one in their circle who calls himself right-wing. Watching the Swede defend himself with his serious voice and glowing eyes, I realized that his right-wing stance is his way of distinguishing himself from all the other Volvo people around him who live in Ikea homes. If only he could see that his views make him the opposite of original. There are millions of salesmen around the world voting for capitalist, xenophobic, and corrupt parties who will only exploit them in return.

Today, I emailed the editor asking if I could publish the piece under a pseudonym. She said if I did, it would take away from the authenticity of the piece. Normally, she wouldn't allow anyone to do it, but since I come from Turkey, she would respect my decision if I decided to do so.

I googled the journal to see who they published before. I saw Bolaño's name and decided to say yes, put my name under my story, this might be my one and only chance to have my name listed next to Don Roberto before I end up as an underpaid and overworked copywriter in Turkey or a Volvo salesman's housewife in Sweden.

March 7

Berlin

Treasures of the day:
5 euros in Pfand
Deodorant
Shampoo
Toothpaste
2 cents

I found a beer and some other things, too, but in the trash. I wanted to take the beer and give it to a punk on Warschauer Strasse, but then I thought that wouldn't help them in the long run, and I left it in the common kitchen. I should know, after all. On my way home, I realized how motherly this thought was and how late my period is.

I had a beer as soon as I got home.

Then I walked to Kotti to mail my mother chocolates for her birthday and buy something to cook. (I haven't found anything good to eat at the hostel in a while now.) I was a bit tipsy after the beer because I had only eaten my free sandwich all day, so I was walking slowly, at the same pace as the other drunks on Skalitzer Strasse. It felt like a holy day, in a Kotti way.

March 9

I've been hoping to find a full bottle of whiskey for months to give the Swede. Today I finally found a bottle of Jameson in one of the dorm rooms. The guests had all checked out and left and not even opened the bottle!

Other treasures of the day:

1 euro

7 cents

March 14

The Sky

I'm finally flying again after working at the hostel for seven days without a break.

I'm in the same plane with a guest from the hostel. He's sitting right behind me, but we're both avoiding each other. He'd thanked me for emptying the trash in his private room earlier today, but maybe he didn't recognize me in my outside world outfit and face. Maybe he thought I couldn't be who he thought I was. How could a cleaner in Berlin afford a trip to Sweden?

Work was extra annoying today because first, this chubby teen who was a guest on the floor I was cleaning stopped in front of the door of the room I was vacuuming and said, "Hey." I looked back at him. He started singing, "Baby go down, down, down." I didn't know what to do so I slammed the door on his face.

Then at lunch, I had to sit with Mia, who's been in the worst mood lately. A couple of weeks ago, when I was stressed with trying to get the last kitchen done before the end of my shift, she came to me and said, "Leyla, will you follow me please? I will show you something." I followed her into the hallway where she showed me one full trash bag and a couple of empty ones. She said she'd just saved all those empty bags. She wanted to show me how I could have saved so much if I transferred the trash in the trash bins in rooms to one big bag, instead of changing them all. Today at lunch, she was commenting on how I always sign up for the new long shift before anybody else has a chance to. She said she was annoyed, even though she'd never want to take those shifts herself.

What's the point of me writing all of this? Is what really bothers me the fact that Mia goes out of her way to do right by the environment and equality when I've so comfortably paired myself with a conservative man whose biggest dream is to move to America and become a true capitalist without Sweden's socialist principles standing in his way? Or am I trying to distract myself from a scarier question: could I actually be pregnant?

March 15

Gothenburg

The Swede is sleeping still, and I am thinking about love. Do I love him? Does he love me? Is it okay that my love is not evenly distributed in time? Sometimes I feel like I am living somebody else's life here and the true Leyla is unaware of or irrelevant to this relationship. Sometimes I feel that I have finally found my true self and I can love him for the rest of my life. That the Swede is nothing like all those other men in novels or soaps or my mother's imagination. That my life is real.

I feel the same way about Berlin and pretty much everything else. But does it mean it is okay?

Evening

I met the Swede's parents today. His mother cooked a big pike her husband fished out of the ice in the morning. His father took me down to their wine cellar and made me pick a bottle from their special occasions shelf. They told me about how they met (which I already knew), embarrassing stories about the Swede that didn't surprise me at all, and how I had to know that the Swede's political views didn't represent the rest of his family's. They didn't know where he got his ideas. I kept my theory to myself and helped the mother clean up the table as the Swede helped his father set up a new swinging sofa in their winter garden.

We used to have a garden too. My father didn't like fishing, but he was always the one to cook the fish. He loved cutting and cleaning all sorts of meat, which only made me detest him more. How could anyone enjoy the crudest parts of cooking the most? He didn't like to spend time in the garden. He even fought with the flies, cursing at them whenever one came too close. So he wouldn't let us be in the garden either. We had a table and a couple of chairs there because I guess he felt like he had to put something out there, but we never had a meal outside as a family. A few months after he died, my mother and I bought an outdoor sofa like the one the Swedes set up today. We didn't yet know that we would have to sell it in less than a year, together with the house and everything else we once owned.

It didn't feel right to feel so at ease being with a perfect family like the Swede's when I haven't seen my own wounded family in over a year. But I drank a lot, and that put me in a good mood again. So good that when my mother and sister called, I picked it up and introduced them to the Swede and his family. I regretted it immediately, but everybody except me thought it was a great idea to ask each other questions in three languages mixed with alcohol and screen freezes. The Swede's mother told my mother that they loved me, the Swede and I both were in love, happy, and healthy, and my mother shouldn't worry about me at all. My mother started crying. Then, the Swede's mother started crying. When I felt that the Swede might be about to cry as well, I said goodbye in three languages on behalf of everyone.

It's as if I took a hit on the head at the end of high school and woke up here in Sweden, tired and drunk. How else could this be happening to me? After all those escapes, years spent alone in decadence, how else could I find myself holding hands with the Swede as our mothers cried out of happiness? I wish I could say the whole incident made me nauseated and I realized I had been faking it, this whole love thing, that all these people were crazy, and I would never come back here. But the Turkish housewife in me never felt happier.

March 17

The Sky

In my dream, I was pregnant. I wanted to get an abortion but then decided to keep it. Then, I regretted not having it aborted before it was too late and was considering potential ways I could kill my baby before it was born, weighing the possibility of the action and the guilt that would follow in consequence and the mass of all the future Leylas I would be killing by having the baby. I woke up before I could make up my mind. I was finally bleeding.

The flight was delayed (again) so I had no excuse not to pick up when my mother called. She told me how much she liked the Swede and his family. I told her that I liked them, too, but our relationship was not as serious as it seemed yesterday on the call. That we wanted two opposite futures from life. She said he was kind, he was handsome, and he was Swedish, so why not compromise for once? I told her that I had to get on the plane and hung up when in fact boarding didn't start for another hour.

I love the Swede. I do. But why is everyone else so enthusiastic about me settling down with him? Just because he's Swedish or because he's kind, handsome, *and* Swedish? What about our worldviews? What about the adventurous writer's life I've risked so much to create for myself? Don't I deserve to be with someone who reads, writes, or at least thinks like me?

Wouldn't they think the Swede was evil for voting right-wing if he were a Turk? Wouldn't they think he was boring for not wanting anything from life other than making money and having kids? How come being from Sweden is enough to make up for all this?

Why is my mother so happy that her daughter is with a Swede when she's never been to Sweden or met a Swede before? When did we internalize their superiority so deeply?

Am I really upset with my mother right now, or am I upset with myself for being unable to say that his Swedishness and stability have nothing to do with how safe and peaceful I feel when I'm with him?

In a world where I've felt unsafe since my conception, is it so wrong to love someone for making me feel like safety could be more than a word in a foreign language?

Is it even possible to separate love from safety and romance from capitalism for anyone in a world where we're forced to use our bodies and thoughts as capital?

If Mona came back to Berlin and asked me to marry her for a visa so we could live and turn tricks happily ever after, would I ever allow myself to have feelings for someone like the Swede?

If I earned enough money to go out with my friends whenever I wanted, would I still choose to spend all my off days in sparkling white Gothenburg, so far from Berlin? Would I feel so at home with the Swede if I didn't?

Nazlı Koca

It's too late for the answers to matter now.
But is love a good enough reason to pair myself with
my antithesis?

March 19

Berlin

Victor and I had five strangers from WG-Gesucht over in our apartment today to choose Heidi's replacement. Victor only responded to people who had their Schufa ready, a high salary and/or wealthy parents who would cosign the lease. If I were a newcomer to Berlin looking for a room, there would be no way I'd be invited to view our flat. Neither would Victor. We both came here with next to nothing. I wanted to try and talk Victor out of turning our home into a Mitte WG, but it seemed futile.

The first stranger was a thirtysomething American jazz guitarist who had just moved to Berlin. He had neither a Schufa nor a job, but he had 20,000 euros saved up. He had lied about having the documents on his profile to be able to pass through WG-Gesucht's filters. He was sitting right across Victor, with me in the middle of the table. I could see Victor's face strain in frustration after this confession, but the guitarist didn't seem to realize or care. He grabbed Alexa from the shelf she was resting on and showed her to us, as if he found a bug that spies had planted in our apartment.

"There's an Alexa here," he said.

"Yes, we know," Victor said.

"Oh," said the guitarist. "I would expect a Cuban programmer and a Turkish writer to care more about their privacy."

"What do you know about being Cuban or Turkish?" Victor asked.

It's for moments like this that I never gave up on our friendship.

The second stranger was a twenty-four-year-old girl from Brazil who spent more time talking about Berghain than anything else. She had been living in Berlin for six months and would stay until her MBA was over, which her father was paying for, as he would be paying her rent and cosigning the lease. After she left, Victor said she was too spoiled.

"What did you expect?" I asked him.

He changed the subject.

The third and fourth strangers were variations of the Berghain girl with minor differences. The final stranger was Laura, a German lawyer in her late twenties. She said she would mostly be away on business trips and sleep at her boyfriend's when in Berlin. She wanted to have a room of her own, just in case.

"Perfect," said Victor.

Perfect.

March 20

Kreuzberg feels dirtier every time I come back from Sweden, every U-Bahn trip more like a chapter from *Naked Lunch*. I wonder what living in a seaside town in Turkey would be like. No, I take that back.

March 22

I read three excerpts about the Swede. I drank a lot, of course, and snuck out without talking to anyone after I read. I didn't take my "donation" either. I woke up to messages from Eve and Eloise asking where I went.

There were about thirty people in the audience. Julia from the dinner at Eve's was there. Ash too. And Colin. But no one else I knew. Before I went up onstage, a Turkish girl in her early twenties who still looked more like a part of Istanbul than Berlin introduced herself to me. She said she heard me read last month and had to come back for more.

"Is this really your diary or a writing project?" she asked.

(I don't remember in which language.)

I told her I didn't know anymore.

Everything I've read onstage was from this diary, yes. But they were curated. I would never read what I wrote about my father or Mona and the secret we share. I haven't even told the Swede about them. But my mind always keeps their skulls at an arm's reach, whether I read, write, or talk about them or not. My father's crime, my secrets, and fears always find a way to take over when I least expect them to, like they did on the stage last night. I was reading my carefully selected, edited, and expanded diary entries about the Swede, but between each sentence I was thinking about everything I've been hiding from the people around me. I couldn't believe that I'd willingly gone up on that stage, as if I were naked in public in a nightmare. So I took bigger sips of my wine after each section, and I ran off as soon as I could, like I always do.

March 23

Warschauer Strasse, I heard a voice in my head say today, as I walked it down from work to the U-Bahn. It was me, talking to myself, but I sounded like Can Dündar, Turkey's household documentarist. I heard about all historical events that were left out of schoolbooks from his deep, serious voice. My whole generation did. TV channels would broadcast his documentaries at every national holiday. He's a political refugee in Berlin now, chased out by the Turkish government to exile for exposing an arms shipment to Islamist Syrian rebels. His exile is the kind that makes my self-exile seem hedonistic, greedy.

My Can Dündar voice continued, *The East Side Shopping Mall was growing more flesh and bone every day, gaining its strength to cannibalize the last bones of communism. What did this mean for Friedrichshain, Berlin, Europe?* I quickly turned left, toward the station. I wanted to give the copper coins I found while cleaning today to the buskers playing at the entrance, but I worried they would be offended. (I think I'm the only one who actually uses cents.) (I always justify not giving money to anyone on the streets by thinking I am poorer than they are.)

I entered the station. A middle-aged man was cleaning the empty U-Bahn. I told myself, in the documentarist's voice: *They are the real Sisyphuses of this city. Berlin will never be cleaned.*

I made the same mistake I always do. I walked all the way down to the last car to be closer to the exit when I arrived at my stop. I remembered why it was a mistake when I saw the regulars of that car: the man who sleeps loudly inside his sleeping bag and the girl who always speaks to herself in German. What if, I thought, she's been speaking to me all these months? Then I decided against it.

Because it's always easier to think they're talking to themselves, I heard my Can Dündar voice narrate me to me. *So Leyla did that again and walked up to the third car from the last.*

I couldn't get this voice out of my head until I came back to my room and started writing. I looked at everyone as if I were a camera and a voice-over commentator. I wrote thoughts into their heads, stories about their lives, anecdotes from their days just by seeing them for a few seconds. And I believed them.

The old Turkish man counting the beads of his tesbih was worrying about his business. The young Syrian man holding his girlfriend's hand was trying to convince her she didn't need to be jealous, because he loved her. The German man holding a book open wasn't actually reading it but instead trying to decide if he wanted to cook tonight or buy a kebab on his way home.

Leyla was wondering if she still made sense there, here, in this city. Or was it time to leave like a good immigrant novelist and write about her once-free existence from a suffocating distance like Raif Efendi in Madonna in a Fur Coat? *Maybe then, years later when she dies in Turkey, a younger clerk in her office job would find her diary in her desk drawer and publish it with a prologue about how unnoteworthy he'd always thought her life must have been.*

Was it possible to live and narrate a story at once without sacrificing one or the other to censorship?

March 27

In my dream, I was using a spy cam to secretly photograph the other cleaners at the hostel. I got caught, but I don't remember by whom.

I cleaned for six hours a day five days in a row. I made 160 beds and cleaned 50 toilets and 17 showers. The right side of my back hurts when I try to hold a wine bottle.

Mona's back in France. She called last night. She said that she spent four weeks at a psychiatric hospital shortly after we spoke in January. She checked herself in because she felt if she hadn't, she'd have done something bad. I wanted to ask what she meant by that, how bad, but I didn't.

"When I left the hospital," she said, "the au pair agency told me that I no longer had a job. The family I'd been working for had already packed my things and sent them to the agency's headquarters, where I had a ticket back home waiting for me."

She's been an au pair all this time! I've thought of a hundred scenarios for what she could be doing, from being a full-time sugar baby to a high-class escort, from being in love with someone she'd hidden from me to going to school in a field she never told me she was into, but it had never occurred to me that she could willingly take care of a baby for $400 a month, food, and shelter.

"Berlin was going to kill me if I stayed any longer," she said. "I couldn't keep up with the drugs and tricks being everywhere all the time in Berlin, wherever I went, even when I didn't want them."

She did always love babies. "I only feel calm when I'm around them," she'd say. "I just want someone to get me pregnant and then disappear."

Her first six months as an au pair were eerily peaceful she told me. The father was mostly away for business, and the mother was always at work. She was a divorce lawyer. Mona thought they were scared of their baby. But she adored him. He was only six weeks old when they met and so smart already! He barely ever cried, as if he felt that he scared his mother and tried not to. The family lived in a small house near a small park. Mona would take the baby there every day and listen to other nannies talk about their problems. She didn't say much. She didn't have any problems. She started dating a nice boy who worked at the coffee shop near the park. She told him about her past, hoping that coming clean to *someone* would make her life feel more real. And it did—until her reality turned into a nightmare. First, the father got laid off and started staying home every day, doing nothing. The couple then laid their cleaner off to save money but kept Mona since she was the cheapest commodity they had. They started serving Mona less meat and stopped offering her a glass of their expensive wine at dinner. But that wasn't what ruined Mona's perfect life. It was the father and how he sat around doing nothing all day. All day, he sat on the corner seat of the sofa and watched TV. When it was time to make breakfast, he did nothing. When it was time to clean up, he did nothing. Lunch, nothing. Dinner, cleaning, trash day—nothing! When the baby cried, he did nothing. And when the mother cried about it one day, begging him to either find a job or to help out with the chores, he yelled at her.

"Guess what he called her?" Mona asked me.

"Whore."

"Whore. You should have seen how embarrassed she was. She was begging me to leave the room with her eyes. The man didn't care that I was there, witnessing his crudeness. It was he who spent her money, yet he called her a whore with such despicable confidence that it was the mother, the woman who felt ashamed of the whole exchange. Every night after that one ended the same. *Jesus. Fuck. Lord. What a fucking whore!* Some evenings the mother cried in her car for hours, unable to enter her own home. I'd watch her from the baby's room upstairs. It all felt too familiar, Leyla, so familiar that it was comfortable. She even looked like my mother a little."

She wanted to help the mother. She knew that she wouldn't leave her husband. She loved him too much. So, Mona accepted her fate. The only way to make the mother's life a little easier was to help out with the housework. And before she knew it, she was their live-in, unpaid, invisible cleaner, in addition to being their live-in, $400, invisible au pair. They seemed to be fighting less. But now Mona couldn't stop fighting the father in her head. Everything he did annoyed her. The way he held the remote control on his belly when he watched TV. The way he smelled of sweat, beer, and onions all the time. How easily he got used to giving her orders.

Even holding the baby didn't stop Mona from spiraling to the point that she started to imagine ways to save the family from the father. What if she seduced him and exposed him to the mother as the worthless pig he was? No, that wouldn't work. The mother would send her away too. What if she stopped cleaning and cooking for them? No, that wouldn't work either. They'd gotten too used to Mona's new role. There was no going back from the role she volunteered to play in their lives. She'd become so absorbed by her hatred of this man that she could no longer stand being around any men, including her boyfriend, whose calls she stopped answering without explanation. She stopped going to the park so she wouldn't run into him. She had too much work to do in the house anyway.

At first, the boyfriend sent her emotional emails professing his love and concern for her well-being. "I just want to know that you're okay. You don't have to be with me. Tell me you're safe and healthy, and I'll leave you alone," he'd write. But after a couple of weeks, his tone changed 180. "You fucking whore," he wrote. "I'm going to tell your employers what you are. I'm not one of your old tricks! You can't get rid of me so easily."

And so Mona's imaginary fights with the father were replaced with the fear of being exposed. She couldn't sleep for days, wondering what the family would do if they found out. Would they notify the agency? Would the agency tell the police? Would they send her back to France? What would happen to the baby if she left? Who'd play with him? Who'd rock his bed when his parents fought?

"When I realized that I couldn't separate myself from the baby, our stories, and our emotions, I went to the hospital to see an emergency therapist. But they wanted me to stay there for a couple of nights. A couple of nights turned to a couple of weeks, and you know the rest."

Did I know the rest? Could I know what she'd been through at the hospital, the little details that pushed her over that edge, how she had to face them to get out? Maybe. I did feel, in her voice, that she knew the confrontations and compromises I've been negotiating within. I felt she knew all my thoughts better than I did.

Once again, I was about to lose myself in her story.

"How did we end up here?" I asked her.

She said, "Je ne sais pas." As if to say, you and I are not in the same place. I'm in another country, languages away from you, Leyla.

March 29

The Swede's sleeping in my bed. I have to go to work soon.

Last night, we celebrated his grandmother Alice's eightieth birthday at Hard Rock Cafe. Yes, his whole family came to Berlin, to go to Hard Rock Cafe.

Alice has a lung disease that has turned her into a child, just like my father. She is an alcoholic, just like me. And my father. It was too painful to talk to her sober, so I drank a lot. Everybody drank a lot.

My father had survived the car crash and three years in prison. Three years spent seeing him through a glass window, watching him shrink and crumple. Three short years that were not enough to pay for what he did, but enough to give him a lung disease that would kill him six months after he got out.

His doctor likened his disease to autumn. His lungs were trees bound to lose their leaves one by one, but we couldn't believe it would be his last spring. Even when we could see all his bones through his skin as he breathed through a ventilator. His release from prison was supposed to be the start of a new life. He was supposed to make amends with the world. And he tried. He stopped drinking and worked long hours every day to save his struggling business. He never raised his hand again. Instead, he teared up often, saying how much he loved us. For the first time, he told us about his childhood. How his father drank himself to death but not before he gambled all their money away and caused my grandmother's first stroke. How all his brothers followed their father's path and how he'd wanted nothing more from life than to avoid the same fate. *I failed*, his watery eyes said. *But I know you won't.* His body gave up on him just when I was beginning to forgive him.

March 31

I went to a concert at Giovanni's last night. I hadn't seen him since autumn, but Giovanni didn't seem to realize how long I'd been gone from his life. I thought he'd be upset with me for vanishing without explanation, but he welcomed me with kisses and ciao bellas and amore mios. He made me a negroni and introduced me to his new boyfriend as "Leyla, the best writer in Berlin," even though he's never read anything I've written or come to any of my readings.

Time seemed to have passed expansively in Giovanni's Room while I've been cleaning the rooms of strangers, sleeping in the Swede's room in Gothenburg, and writing in my room, looking inward for the last six months. Giovanni didn't find a new host for my show like I feared. He found new acts to put on for those who wanted to look outward. Out onto the stage in search of beauty and excitement. As I sipped my negroni and told him about my forthcoming publication, my readings at Atwood, and my escapades to Sweden, I realized I wasn't as ready as I thought to be back there. The flip side of my story kept bugging me, but I didn't know how to weave my bleak circumstances into the narrative of the brilliant writer Giovanni saw me as. Not when I was standing so close to the stage where I once thirstily expected others to do so.

The concert was of a German duo who combined classical music with techno and live screams. While they played, a Russian ballerino dressed all in black walked among the audience, touching people's faces, closing and opening their eyes and mouths. At first, I thought he'd do it to a couple of people in the front row and stop, but he was not skipping anyone, so I left the room when he came too close to my seat.

When I got home, I caught Victor cooking in the kitchen and begged him to watch an episode of *Amor prohibido* with me.

"Okay but only one episode," he said. We watched the final one, in which Bihter shoots herself in the heart because Behlül, the man she had an affair with, who also happens to be the nephew of her husband, is getting married to her stepdaughter, Nihal. Hours before the wedding, she takes a shower, puts on a white dress, and takes her husband's gun from the safe. Behlül storms into the room and asks her to stop. Bihter tells Behlül that he is killing her to save Nihal. "Why *me*?" she asks. "Beni, beni, Bihterini? Por qué yo?"

While we were watching this scene, I imagined a couple of dramatic acts in my head. In the first one, I was two Leylas, and one Leyla said to the other, "Beni, beni . . ."

In another one, Victor asked me, "Why the Swede? Why are you surrendering to him of all people? You fought so hard for your freedom. Don't do it."

Then I told him, "Because of you! Because you surrendered to the system first! If you hadn't left me all alone, none of this would be happening!"

In real life, Victor said he had to go back to work, so I returned to my room and typed *Amor prohibido* in the search bar.

Aşk-ı Memnu, as it is called in Turkish, is a modern-day adaptation of one of the first novels written in Turkey. It was serialized in a literary journal in the nineteenth century. The first TV series ever made in Turkey was a black-and-white adaptation of *Aşk-ı Memnu* as well. So, the one Victor and I watched is an adaptation of an adaptation, dubbed in Spanish, and subtitled in English. Apparently a US-based channel did an adaptation of the adaptation of the adaptation too. They called it *Pasión prohibida,* filmed in Miami, and cast Mónica Spear, a Venezuelan beauty queen, as Bihter. Mónica was murdered in an armed robbery while she was in Venezuela with her daughter and ex-husband the summer after the first season.

So much translation, adaptation, transformation—what for? Death conquers all versions, all stories.

Except *in* the soap realm. Soaps suggest alternative realities in which death is not absolute, as opposed to life, where death hits you like a truck hits a bird on the highway and is followed by hundreds of cars driving over its guts so there's no trace of it left on the cement by the end of the day.

As a soap viewer, you can anticipate a resurrection of your favorite character. *They didn't really die. They'll come back in the season finale* you can speculate. No big deal. Even if the actor who played that character dies in real life, there's still hope for the character to come back with a new face after having gone under a series of aesthetic surgeries to fake his own death and protect his family.

Since my father died, I've dreamed of his return to life in every scenario soaps claimed plausible, but he was always gone when I woke up. And, to stay sane, I had to remind myself how I kissed his cold, yellowing face in the mosque before his funeral, on the icy stone where his body lay between me, my sister, my mother, and the imam. How our cries and the imam's prayers echoed in the room, but my father remained dead quiet. How tight I held the earth in my right hand until it was my turn to throw it onto his grave.

I wish I'd stayed at the event at Giovanni's and waited for the ballerino to touch my face so I could scream back at him. Now it feels like a dozen silent screams got stuck in my throat, like fish bones.

I feel on the verge of making a terrible mistake, but I don't know what it will be.

April 2

Last night, for the first time in months, my father came to my sleep to visit me. Or should I say I visited him? He had a grocery store on Karl Marx Strasse. It was cold. He was colder. I was freezing. He told me I could take home whatever I wanted.

Olive oil soap, raki, lemon cologne. The store had all his favorite things—and none of mine.

I told him I needed his help with my visa.

He said he couldn't help me with that. He didn't have a visa either. He was still waiting for his visa to get into hell.

Does this mean I will know what to do with my life once I accept that he's in hell? Or that he'll go to hell when I figure out what to do? Or that he doesn't necessarily belong in hell? Or that I don't belong here?

Then where *do* we belong?

April 5

At my college graduation ceremony, the CEO of the biggest company in Turkey gave the keynote speech. He said, "Make sure you do your best in every job you have. Be it a simple internship or running a large company. Remember, you'll be leaving your mark behind in each role you take." Well, I will obviously never run a company like his. And I don't think he ever had to clean a hostel bathroom in his life.

After work today, I got this message from the head of the maids through the app: *Lela, you have been working here for months, but yesterday you forgot to clean a room! How? This not a detail but your main task!? When a couple checked into the 300 yesterday, their was of course a big problem! Their have been more complaints about your work before. I warned you, you will remember. I'm going to on vacation today, but when I get back we talk. Please think weather you can rieely improve so that you can continue working here and weather this job suits you!*

I doubt that I actually skipped a room. There must have been an error in the system or something, but it could also be true because let's be honest, it does sound like something I could do. I told her okay, I quit. I'll stop working at the end of May. I won't need this job after I receive that last paycheck anyway. Either a miracle will happen and I will figure out the rest, or my Fiktionsbescheinigung will expire and I'll have to leave Berlin.

I called the Swede and told him I was fired. He didn't think the head of the maids was firing me in her message.

"But maybe it was for the best," he said. "Don't worry about the visa too much. Even if you have to go back to Turkey, you can apply for a Swedish visa to come live with me in Gothenburg as my partner. We don't need to be married to get you a visa in Sweden. All we have to do is declare we're in a relationship and want to live together."

"You have to wait for that visa in your home country for two years, whether you're married or partners, and some people still don't get it," I said. "I would lose my mind in Turkey if I had to stay there for two years."

He didn't believe me.

"I'm a Swedish citizen," he said. "It can't be that difficult to bring my girlfriend to my own country."

Westerners never understand how immigration works for people who are from unwanted countries. Turkish citizens need to apply and pay for visas just to set foot in the airport of a European country as a tourist. Even then, we can be sent back, if the officer has a hunch that we're a threat. To get that visa one must show a fortune in a bank account or a stable and sufficient source of income, a luxury only a handful of us have.

"Come here," he said. "Let's look into it together."

I told him I'd think about it and spent the next two hours typing and deleting this text:

"What if there are things about me, things I've done in the past, that may have changed your mind about committing to a partnership with me, but I might never tell you?"

He texted back immediately:

"My love, what you did in the past is none of my business."

Then:

"As long as you didn't kill anyone."

And then:

"You didn't kill anyone, right?"

I didn't reply.

Half an hour later, I got a text from Scandinavian Airlines, telling me I had a flight to Sweden tomorrow night.

April 8

Gothenburg

The Swede is at work. I spent most of the day on the couch, eating chocolate-covered almonds, drinking the Sangiovese his mother gave us, listening to Schubert's "Serenade" on repeat, and reading *After Kathy Acker* by Chris Kraus (which cost the Swede 300 Swedish kronur). I had been looking forward to reading this book ever since I read *I Love Dick* last year, and until I finished reading the last page, I thought it was the best biography I'd ever read. Then, I closed its hardcover, got my head up, saw my reflection on the TV screen, and felt chills all over my body.

I'd made a Sylvia Plath–themed zine once, put a photograph of her gravestone taken by Patti Smith on the cover, and I crossed "Hughes" out of Plath's name on the headstone with a gold marker. I got the same kind of chill after I did that, too, and felt as though Sylvia were telling me to mind my own business, that she died as the wife of the man she loved no matter what.

This one was a revelation from Acker. I got off the couch and started walking around in the apartment, flipping through the book in my head. I loved reading the book, true. How could I not? I've loved everything about Acker since Mona first told me about her. She'd gifted me a copy of *Blood and Guts in High School* on my birthday, and I had devoured it. True, that was another Leyla, eating up yet another Leyla, crushing, chewing, swallowing herself with sex, drugs, and violent literature. But a more recent Leyla had read *I Love Dick* in a few sittings. These two women, Acker and Kraus, wrote so fiercely about being wired to desire men who frustrated them that I thought I could use their fictions as manuals how not to surrender to love. But I saw on the TV screen how today I, too, like Kraus, was thinking of Acker as a bleak story, an angry lone wolf. Acker had not stuck with any of her lovers. She moved around a lot instead. She didn't trust modern medicine. She died single, without many close friends. She died at fifty, when Chris Kraus lived to be sixtysomething and married Sylvère Lotringer, to whom Kathy Acker once wrote that she only felt alive when they fucked.

But so what? Didn't they also separate at the end, after Kraus spent her youth following her husband around, sitting by his side as he talked about his projects to men who didn't care what Kraus had to say? She wrote so herself. How could she write this book the way she did then, claiming to come from a place of admiration, but slowly weaving a narrative in which Acker is revoked as a jealous, hysterical, desperate bitch?

Night

I had to stop writing when I heard the Swede's keys unlock the door.

He walked in saying, "Hello love." I felt an equal repulsion and compulsion to say it back, so I didn't. I hesitated to walk over and kiss him like I always do. He asked what was wrong and I told him all about the book, Acker, Kraus, Lotringer, even Plath and Hughes as he took off his suit and hung it up on the door of his gaming dungeon.

"Sounds like someone's jealous of her husband's ex," he said.

I didn't like hearing that from him. It didn't feel right for a man to simplify Kraus like that.

"But what do I know," he said as though he knew what I was thinking. "I haven't heard of any of those people before. You're the smart one. You tell me. Why did it bother you so much?"

He asked this so lightly, as if we were talking about an annoying client or something a manager said at work that would be forgotten the next day.

He couldn't care less about Acker's life choices. He wouldn't judge me for being unfair to the other if I chose to like or dislike the book. In fact, no one would, no one that should matter at least, except myself.

When I put them in the same room with the Swede, all my intellectual questions dissolve.

If he told me one day that he would rather stay childless with me than be with anyone else, would it be possible then to keep this life? Keep thinking the way I do and turn it off to just be when the Swede comes home from work?

Acker would have never settled down with a Volvo salesman who wasn't at least a little bit of a genius and a little dark and twisted in an exciting way. Even Kraus wouldn't have done it.

But what if they didn't have their Western citizenships? What if Kathy didn't inherit all that money from her estranged family? What if she never knew that she would one day? Would she have lived so freely then? She couldn't have done sex work forever. She would have eventually run out of couches to crash on, grants to get. What if she were a citizen of Morocco not America? Would she still be so bold and selective with her lovers, so edgy with her image? Wouldn't she start worrying about retirement instead of buying a motorcycle then? Would she be able to write as radically as she did if she had the Turkish government to worry about?

Maybe so. But maybe not.

The immigration office is called Migrationsverket Nationellt Servicecenter here, meaning "Migration Board National Service Center" and not "Foreigners Authority," like Ausländerbehörde. It was much smaller, and I didn't see anyone who had the unbearable tension on their faces that comes from knowing they have to be at their best to charm angry officers who are more likely to scold them for their life choices and send them away than help them. Or I didn't see my own fear in other people's eyes because I was with the Swede.

We took a number from the machine and sat in the waiting room. We were able to see someone within half an hour. In Berlin, if you don't have an appointment, you'd have to go at 5:00 a.m., get in the line, and consider yourself lucky if you could meet someone before noon. The officer was a welcoming Swede of color and she told us, both in English and Swedish, what I already told the Swede: I'd have to apply from and wait for the results in Turkey and would only be allowed to visit Sweden on short tourist visas until the application would be approved. She said we had a high chance of getting the visa because the Swede owns his own apartment and has a salary enough to cover both of our expenses.

"I had no idea this visa business could be so confusing," he said. "But I'm ready to do this if you are."

It's scary how similar being with the Swede is to being with my mother. How I love them both but can't talk to them about anything I truly care about. How most of my interactions with them are limited to eating together, holding each other, and recaps of the mundane. How much love they both have to give and how I almost feel crushed under it.

If I can consider a future with the Swede, why can't I imagine one with my mother? Am I considering a future with the Swede so that I can acclimate myself to a future in Turkey? If I spend enough time in the Swede's apartment, enough nights falling asleep watching Hollywood movies, enough mornings talking about nothing but food, can I finally give up on Berlin and the dream of writing without fear one day? Can I finally be a good daughter, sister, wife, citizen in Turkey?

Or is this how people give up on themselves? Is this how people die?

April 10

Berlin

Spring is almost here. Kotti is flaming with overdoses, sirens, and ambulances again. On the U1, tourists talk about cherries blossoming in parts of the city I've never seen. I have two months left on my visa.

Today at work, as I cleaned and polished mirrors, sinks, toilet seats, I thought about my chances of staying in Berlin. The court never responded to my request to set a hearing. None of the jobs I applied for got back to me. Even if I risked it all and overstayed my visa, there's no reason to hold on to the idea of home in our overpriced apartment after Heidi and Victor are gone. Where would I live?

What if I went back to Turkey for two years before Gothenburg or for good? How long before people realize I'm not the Leyla they missed? What if the Swede changes his mind in the process? Could I ever become a novelist in Turkey? If I did, how long would it take for me to be put on trial and then in prison for my novels?

All the other cleaners finished their floors before the end of the shift and offered to help so we could all clock out early. They all seemed to know that I got fired for being a lousy cleaner. I quietly handed over my mop, vacuum cleaner, and cart. Left with stinking trash bags in two hands in the middle of the hallway, it occurred to me that the only thing I was fast at was thinking. Still, no matter how many anxious thoughts I could fit into a split second, I knew nothing. I didn't know what else I could do to stay in Berlin. I didn't know the word for home in Swedish. I didn't know what one Turkish lira is worth now against the euro.

So, I switched to playing the final scene from *Uzak* in my mind, in which the main guy who once didn't want the main girl begs her to stay. The camera zooms in on his eyes first, then the girl's. She says yes. Like Molly in *Ulysses*.

April 27

I spent the morning trying to find a doctor who would write me a sick note. I wasn't sick, but I had already set my mind to get a note to cover all my shifts until the end of May. Yes, I know this means truly screwing the other cleaners over. They will have to cover for me for the whole month, including May Day. But if a cleaner on an expiring fictional visa doesn't deserve to be a little bit of an asshole sometimes, then who does?

I could have gone to the clinic in Kotti, but the old Turkish doctor there asked me out last time when I had barely put my clothes back on, so I didn't want to see him. I went to Neukölln. I walked past Scardanelli, the frowning Turkish man's bakery, and my first Berlin apartment.

The Neukölln doctor turned out to be too busy, so I ended up in Kotti again, but the old man wasn't in. My doctor was a young Turkish woman who listened to me curiously as I told her the story of my back injury as if it had happened last week. She wrote me the perfect note. I gave her a soap recommendation.

Back home, first I emailed the head of the maids saying I was in too much pain and was advised not to work for a month. She didn't respond to me but wrote to everybody else on the company app asking who could take over my last shifts.

Then, I set up a fake Facebook account and posted an ad to rent out my room. Not because I'd decided where to go but because I needed to be the one to decide when to leave. I said yes to the first person who wrote to me: an abstract painter from Mexico who moved to Berlin last week. I told her she could have the room at least for a month, maybe keep it forever. Victor and the new roommate would say the last word.

I went down the stairs to look for my faithful black suitcase in the basement, the one I bought in Istanbul five years ago to move my life to Berlin.

But the sunset pulled me outside.

Walking to Görlitzer Park in my bleach-stained pants and slippers, I crossed the street at a red light, even though I could see a car was coming, that it was fast and close. It's not that I didn't care about the driver. It wasn't a suicidal impulse either. It wasn't me. It was my legs that I've pulled around for so long when they didn't have the strength that they didn't know how to stop now, like how I kept spinning that night after Eve fell down. I crossed the street and the driver pressed the horn so long it sounded as if he were my future shouting at me, as if he were Israfil blowing the trumpet, as if he were a mother in labor. All I could do was keep walking.

Every inch of my body has been aching since I got back home, as if that car hit me today.

Or as if I were in the car with my father, as if it'd all happened yesterday.

But I wasn't. I wasn't in that car with him. I am not my father.

We're both escapists, yes. I learned how to live from him. He who lived without realizing escape and freedom aren't the same. He drank to free himself from his immutable anger at life, which only made it louder and put him behind bars.

I, too, thought it was freedom I was after all this time. To break free from the violence that raised me, the legacy of a drunk murderer. It was the opposite. I picked up his punishment where he left off and grew it within all this time, so that I could carry him with me. So that I could escape the certainty of his destruction. Because he was my father, whose love I needed as much as I wanted to hate him. How I resembled him. He'd put alcohol between himself and us, just like I've laid bricks made of secrets between myself and the world. I believed that if I stayed away from my family, I could only hurt myself. I crashed on every wall like a raging bull, until my horns broke and fell, until I became unrecognizable to every herd I was once a part of. Like my mother, I distanced all witnesses to my downfall so I could be alone with my wounds, so no one could touch and burn them.

I thought another country would be far enough. If I didn't speak in Turkish, my grief would eventually stop talking to me. If I didn't write in Turkish, I could create a different life for myself. If I didn't think in Turkish, my past couldn't dictate my future.

I never learned German, so Berlin couldn't read my thoughts. I kept all my friends at a safe distance and pushed them away when I revealed too much. I only attached myself to people who were en route to the exit from the beginning. I fell in love with the Swede, a man so foreign to me he felt like a figment of my imagination. As if by putting layer upon layer between myself and others I could avoid the pain of their inevitable loss.

A forceful wind just filled my room with a whistle announcing the night, then left. I can hear my heart beat now, my pen swaying on the paper. I can feel the disquiet suspending from my ceiling. I hung it up there. I turned my fear into guilt, shame, and secrets, split it into small pieces. I made invisible weapons of self-destruction out of each one and placed them in every corner of my room.

I know now that my weapons never stood a chance against death or life.

It's time to stop capturing ghosts with bottles of wine and making their curses mine. It's time to put my laptop screen down and face the mirror—without the Looking Glass cleaning supplies. It's time to get past the stains and look into my own eyes, no matter how scared they are.

Because I will not stage another coup against myself, another escape.

This time, I will take my story with me, all of it, as I write on the pages of this ugly notebook that I've come to love.

Acknowledgments

Her şeyden önce, teşekkürler anne. İyi ki varsın abla.

Thank you to everyone who opened their homes, hearts, and minds to me while I worked on this novel, especially Sinéad Cerf, Dayna Gross, Kirsten Aguilar, Azareen Van der Vliet Oloomi, and Elif Batuman.

Thank you to Wendy Lesser for being the first to believe in this story. Thank you to Alissa Doroh, Barry McCrea, Johannes Göransson, Steve Tomasula, Valerie Sayers, Olivier Morel, and all the generous scholars at the University of Notre Dame and the University of Denver who almost make me believe that academia could be more than a weapon of ideological warfare. Thank you to Joyelle McSweeney, who suggested I name my novel *The Applicant* after reading my poem with the same title.

Thank you, Sylvia Plath, for writing the original "The Applicant." Thank you to Nina Simone, Müslüm Gürses, Cem Karaca, and all musicians whose songs bled into these pages and gave it life. Thank you to Agnès Varda, Chantal Akerman, Jafar Panahi, and all filmmakers whose lenses cleared Leyla's. Thank you to Kathy Acker, James Baldwin, Roberto Bolaño, and all the writers who guided both Leyla and me all the way here.

Thank you to my agent Elias Altman. Thank you to Elisabeth Schmitz, the most supportive editor I could ask for. Thank you to Yvonne Cha, Lilly Sandberg, Paula Cooper Hughes, Julia Berner-Tobin, Justina Batchelor, Andrew Unger, and everyone at Grove who read and worked on this novel.

Thank you to all printers, warehouse workers, and delivery heroes who will carry these pages on their backs, and to all the booksellers who might receive, shelve, and recommend this novel to its future readers.

Thank you to every single cleaner in this messed up world we live in. I wish you the wildest daydreams and all the luck it takes to make them come true.

And thank you to my awe-inspiring friends in Turkey, Germany, Cuba, France, Sweden, Spain, China, and the US. You are real treasures.